TRUE FRIENDS?

"I'm so excited about Saturday," Jazz said, her blue eyes twinkling.

"I can't wait," Lindsay agreed. "We rented a special party room at Rockin' Rollers and everything. So, what are you going to wear?"

"I don't know," Jazz admitted, now that she had agreed to lend Lindsay her pink dress with the little white bows.

"Guys really like that kind of stuff," Lindsay confided. "Bows, flowers, lace. It's the best way to get a guy to notice you."

"Do you really think so?" Jazz asked.

"Of course," Lindsay said. "Joey says that guys like girls who look like girls. He also said that guys like girls who *act* like girls."

"What's that supposed to mean?" Jazz wanted to know.

"It means that you should quit that dorky baseball team and start acting like one of my friends again. . . ."

THE PINK PARROTS

ALL THAT JAZZ

Created by Lucy Ellis

By B. B. Calhoun

A *SPORTS ILLUSTRATED FOR KIDS* BOOK

Created by Lucy Ellis
Written by B. B. Calhoun
Cover art by Jeff Mangiat
Interior line art by Jane Davila
Produced by Angel Entertainment, Inc.

SPORTS ILLUSTRATED FOR KIDS is a trademark of THE TIME INC. MAGAZINE COMPANY

SPORTS ILLUSTRATED FOR KIDS Books is a joint imprint of Little, Brown and Company and Warner Juvenile Books.

Printed in the United States of America

First Printing: October 1990
10 9 8 7 6 5 4 3 2 1

Published simultaneously in Canada by Little, Brown & Company (Canada) Limited

ISBN 0-316-12445-1
Library of Congress Catalog Card Number: 90-050347

1

Lavender Bouquet Bubble Bath. A bathtub full of steaming hot water and fluffy white bubbles, lightly scented with lavender. A tray balanced across the tub holding seven shades of nail polish, a jar of cleansing mud for a facial and Lavender Bouquet After-Bath lotion. Two huge bath towels warming up in front of the radiator.

Jasmine Jaffe, or Jazz, as she was called by almost everyone, opened her eyes with a sigh. She wasn't in a tub full of bubbles at all. She was still stuck out there in rightfield, waiting for this stupid baseball game to be over. The muddy baseball field was still there in front of her, and the opposing team, Ten Pin Bowling, was still up at bat. And it was still drizzling.

Jazz squinted around the field at the other wet members of the Pink Parrots, the only all-girls baseball team in Emblem (Eastern Maryland Baseball League), but they were all intent on the game. It was the bottom of the fifth and the Pink Parrots were winning against Ten Pin Bowling and the score was 5-4. Ten Pin had runners at first and third with two outs.

Jazz pushed her long and soggy honey blonde hair out of her eyes and felt around in her uniform pants pocket for a ponytail holder so she could at least pull her hair off her face. She had joined the Pink Parrots because her mother had made her join; her cousin, Breezy Hawk, was the team captain and Jazz's mom thought Breezy was practically perfect. Jazz was surprised that she actually kind of liked being on the team even though she had never really played baseball before. The girls were fun, except that they all took the games so seriously. And Ro, their coach and sponsor, was a real trip. She ran the Pink Parrot Beauty Salon and she had the greatest clothes. Ro was always telling Jazz that she would be a good baseball player if only she concentrated on the game. Jazz tried to concentrate, but she wasn't very good at it. The other girls, especially Breezy, got mad at her a lot for not paying attention.

"Ouch!" Jazz yelped all of a sudden as something hard hit her on the leg.

"Get the ball!" Julie yelled from centerfield.

Jazz just stood there looking around for the ball, but she couldn't see it anywhere. Breezy was jumping up and down on the pitcher's mound and yelling something Jazz couldn't hear. Breezy was always yelling. Why didn't she just come out to rightfield and find the ball if she had so much to say about it. All this yelling only made Jazz more nervous. If I was a ball, where would I be, Jazz wondered. And that's when she saw the small gray-white blob in the grass just behind her.

"Come on, Jazz," Crystal, the Parrots' first baseman, a tall black girl who Jazz thought was totally beautiful, called out as Jazz picked up the ball. "Throw it here."

Jazz dropped the ball in her haste to get it to Crystal, so she had to bend down to pick it up again. Finally she got the ball to Crystal, who threw it straight to Breezy. Ten Pin had already scored, however, and now led the Parrots 6-5 in the top of the sixth and final inning. Jazz put her hands on her hips and sighed. She tried to do things right, but there were so many things to remember. She couldn't help it if the ball had just slipped out of her glove. Baseball was so *complicated*.

Suddenly Jazz realized that the rest of her team was headed back to the dugout. Breezy must have struck the next Ten Pin batter out. Her cousin was an incredible pitcher, that was for sure. Jazz trotted in behind the others, her sneakers squooshing in the mud with every step. She took her place on the bench with the rest of the Pink Parrots. Their coach, Rose Anne DiMona (but always called Ro), was waiting in the dugout for them. Somehow, Ro's big, major hair had managed to stay up half a foot or so above her head even though it was drizzling. Today, Ro was wearing the hot pink Pink Parrots' team jersey over a pink and purple long-sleeved tie-dyed shirt. Her hot pink biker shorts matched the pink in her shirt perfectly. And Jazz loved Ro's hot pink sneakers. With her big hair, long neon pink nails and wild clothes, Ro didn't look like any other coach in Emblem.

Jazz thought Ro was a great coach. Ro knew baseball

inside and out. Her father had been a minor leaguer who had made it to the big time for two whole weeks, and Ro's brother was playing minor league baseball right now. Ro's training methods, like her hairstyles and clothes, were pretty radical, but Ro wanted the Pink Parrots to be the best team in the league. Jazz didn't have a clue if they ever would be—she didn't even know what their standing was now—but Ro was determined. She said if she could open her own salon in the middle of Maryland, even though all of her family and friends in New Jersey said she couldn't, then surely the Pink Parrots could win the league championship.

Ro put her hands on her hips and began pacing back and forth in front on the bench, snapping her gum as she walked. Jazz knew that this meant that they were in for a talk. Ro loved to give the team pep talks all the time.

"*Team!*" Ro began. "Let's talk."

Jazz sighed. She loved to talk, but about boys and clothes and stuff, not about baseball.

"We are not going to let this get us down!" Ro announced, bouncing up and down enthusiastically as she spoke. "Because this game is not over yet, and I know we can still do it. They are only up by one run. We can win this game."

Jazz felt all eyes were upon her, so she looked down at her dirty Keds. She knew it was her fault Ten Pin had gotten that run, and she was sorry and everything, but she couldn't do anything about it now. Why couldn't they lighten up already?

"Jazz," Breezy said gruffly, her black eyes blazing.

"You've got to keep your eye on the ball."

"O.K., O.K.," Jazz mumbled, twisting a damp strand of her hair around one finger.

"To win, you know we have to get two runs," Julie McKay, the second baseman, pointed out. "And it's raining, and they're putting in Chris Lavery, their star reliever, against us."

"So?" Breezy said, wrinkling her forehead and pressing her lips together, the way she always did when she was mad. Breezy hadn't even noticed the steady trickle of water that was running off the end of her dirty blonde ponytail and down her back.

But Kim Yardley, the red-headed shortstop, and Breezy's best friend, spoke up instead. Kim was just as crazy about baseball as Breezy was, but she never lost patience with anyone. "We've got a chance to get that run back and still win the game," Kim said with an encouraging smile. "Chris Lavery is not perfect."

Jazz looked over at the boys from Ten Pin Bowling, who were taking their places on the field. Chris Lavery, the handsome, auburn-haired pitcher was warming up on the mound. He looked pretty perfect to her.

"O.K., Kim, you're up first," Ro said, looking at her clipboard. "Let's get something started!"

Jazz watched as Kim grabbed a bat and helmet and headed back into the rain. She thought Kim was so cute with her red hair and freckles. And the guys were always picking her up, literally, and kidding around with her and calling her Shorty. Kim was one of the nicest people in the world.

"Come on, Kim," Breezy yelled, as Kim stepped into the batter's box and flung her red braids over her shoulder.

"Go get 'em, Kim!" called Terry DiSunno, pulling her catcher's equipment off. She took off her hat and squeezed the water out of her long, brown hair.

"Hey!" Jazz yelled at her friend. "You're getting my feet wet!" She pointed at her sneakers, where the water from Terry's hair was running.

"Sor-ry!" Terry apologized, exaggerating the syllables. "I forgot that you melt when you get wet, unlike the rest of us."

Kim wiped her hands on her uniform pants. She lifted the bat to her shoulder. As usual, when Kim was really concentrating, the tip of her tongue stuck out of her mouth. Chris Lavery went into his windup.

Kim let the first pitch go by—it was low. "Ball one!" the umpire screamed out.

The next pitch whizzed right down the middle, but Kim swung at it and missed. She caught a piece of the third pitch and popped it up over the pitcher's head. Kim sprinted up the base path, but the second baseman caught the ball and she was out.

Kim looked really frustrated as she walked back to the bench. Jazz couldn't understand that. It was just a baseball game. She, Jazz, had never, ever gotten a hit, not even in practice, but she never got totally upset about it. She had made a great catch in the game last week against Mitchell Lumber. It was the last out of the last inning and the Parrots had won. Jazz remembered that it had felt pretty cool to make that catch. But still, it wasn't the end of the world when she struck out.

Breezy was gritting her teeth. Jazz thought she looked pretty frustrated, too. Breezy had made the last out in the fifth when she had come about two feet short of a home run, and chances were she wouldn't get to bat in this inning. Jazz could tell that Breezy would do anything to step into the batter's box right now. She wondered if her cousin could switch places with her if she had to bat in this inning. Jazz couldn't care less, and she could even stay out of the rain that way.

Terry was up next. She took a few practice swings and finally settled the bat on her shoulder. As she dug in she gave Chris Lavery her monster look, the nasty face she always made to scare off pitchers. She flared her nostrils, puffed up her cheeks and glared. A husky big-boned girl, Terry could be very scary when she did that.

Chris's first pitch was a fastball, which Terry fouled off. At least Breezy said it was a fastball. Jazz had no idea what the difference was between a fastball, a change-up, a split-finger fastball or any of those other pitches. They all came at her when she was up and she missed all of them. Jazz turned back to the game. Terry stepped out of the batter's box, took a deep breath and slowly stepped back in. She swung her bat the whole time.

Terry connected on the next pitch, tapping the ball over the first baseman's head for a single.

"All right, Terry!" Breezy called, jumping up in excitement. "Way to go!"

Jazz cheered, along with all the other Parrots, as Terry

ran to first. Then she took off her hat and pushed her wet hair off her face again. For the hundredth time that day she wished she had brought an elastic with her so she could put her hair in a ponytail. When she asked her cousin for one, Breezy just told her that was what she got for being vain. Jazz didn't know what Breezy meant by that. She shook her head and tried to get her mind back on the game. She looked toward the batter's box and tried to remember how many outs there were.

Sarah Fishman, who played centerfield and pitched, was up at bat. Jazz knew that Sarah wasn't a slugger like Terry or anything, but she was definitely better than Betsy, who was the second worst next to Jazz. Jazz was the worst—she had never gotten a single hit ever, not even in practice. Breezy said that this wasn't humanly possible, but Jazz was living proof.

"Go get 'em, Sarah," yelled Breezy, standing up next to Jazz and clenching her fists. "Show 'em what you've got!"

"Yay, Sarah!" Jazz echoed. Jazz was a great cheerleader. Jazz watched as the first pitch hit the dirt in front of the plate. "Ball one!" the umpire called out.

Squinting her blue eyes at Chris, Jazz decided that he looked really cute now that he had his brown hair cut really short on the sides and he had gotten contact lenses. She had known him since kindergarten, but looking at him now in his uniform, as he went into his windup, Jazz thought he seemed older somehow and more masculine or something.

The next pitch was wide. Sarah caught a piece of it and

popped it up somewhere between first and second base. The second baseman dropped the ball, Terry advanced to second and Sarah was safe at first.

The Parrots all cheered and Ro jumped up and down in excitement. Jazz began to wonder what color she should polish her nails after she got out of her Lavender Bouquet Bubble Bath. She had begun collecting nail polish back in fifth grade. Now she had more than 30 different colors. At the beginning of the school year, Lindsay Cunningham, one of Jazz's best friends and probably the most popular girl at the Eleanor Roosevelt Junior High School, had made a pact with her friends never to wear the same color for two days in a row. Jazz had loved the idea. But that had been before baseball, before the Pink Parrots. Now it was so hard to keep her nails looking nice. They were always breaking inside her glove. Lindsay wasn't very understanding about this. She always told Jazz that girls weren't supposed to play baseball anyway. Jazz didn't really agree with Lindsay about that. Breezy had played for as long as she could remember. And Ro loved to play. But on days like this, Jazz wondered if Lindsay might be right.

Now there was one out and it didn't look good for the Pink Parrots. Jazz was deep in thought about her nails. She had narrowed her decision to a choice between Mildly Mauve and Bashful Blush. Ro suddenly pounded Jazz on the back, startling her.

"Come on, Jazz, get with the program!" Ro said, raising her eyebrows and smiling. "You're up." Ro cracked her gum and handed Jazz a batting helmet.

Jazz blinked. She had just decided on Bashful Blush and here she was putting on this ugly, old batting helmet instead.

"Come on, Jazz, this is it," said Andrea Campbell, who played third base.

This was what, Jazz wondered.

She felt someone give her a little shove. Jazz turned around. It was Breezy. "Give it all you've got, Jazz," her cousin said, pushing her out of the dugout. "This is our last chance."

Oh, no, thought Jazz, suddenly realizing what was happening. It was the bottom of the sixth inning, there was one out, Terry was on second base and Sarah was on first. And it was Jazz's turn at bat. Jazz had gotten on base only once before when she had been marched . . . no, that wasn't right . . . walked. She had been walked. Well, she'd have to try to walk now, she just didn't remember exactly what she had done that other time.

Jazz picked up a bat and walked to the plate in a daze. She felt cold and wet as soon as she got out into the drizzle again. Her thick, matted hair felt like a wet lump on her back. She took a deep breath, stepped up to the plate and lifted the bat to her shoulder.

"Come on, Jazz!" Terry called from second. "Just get on base! Keep us alive!"

Jazz nodded uncertainly. That was easy for Terry to say—she had gotten plenty of hits. But Jazz was the strikeout queen of the Pink Parrots.

"Hey, Jazz!" called Ro from the bench. "You're standing too close to the plate. Try to back up a little!"

Jazz took a step back and planted her feet in the mud. Her white Keds would never be clean again.

"Jazz!" Terry called out. "Your hands are reversed! Put the right one on top!"

Jazz switched her hands and took a deep breath. She squeezed her eyes shut for a moment and wished as hard as she could that she would hit the ball. She had gone through this wishing routine every time she was up at bat. It had never worked before, but that didn't prove anything. Hitting the ball didn't really mean that much to her, but she hated to see how upset the rest of the Parrots got every time she struck out.

Jazz opened her eyes again. She knew she was supposed to concentrate and look at the pitcher, but all she could think about was how cute he was. Jazz definitely did not want him to see her like this—all wet and disgusting. So maybe if she didn't look at him, he wouldn't look at her. And Ro always said to keep your eye on the *ball*, so she'd just wait until the pitch got really close to her and then look up.

Jazz took a deep breath and waited. Whatever happened, she figured, she would be in that Lavender Bouquet Bubble Bath pretty soon.

The first pitch whizzed by her. Jazz didn't even see it. She heard it hit the catcher's mitt and then the umpire yelled, "Strike one!"

"Keep your eye on the ball!" Breezy called from the bench.

Jazz squinted her blue eyes in concentration. She was really going to try to get a hit. This time when the ball

11

got into her field of vision, she swung. She missed the pitch by a good foot and she swung the bat so hard that she spun around. Her feet got tangled up and she fell down, right in the mud. She heard everyone screaming suddenly. What, no one ever fell down before, she thought angrily. It must happen a lot. She struggled to her feet with as much dignity as possible and noticed that David Tabb, the catcher, was scrambling around by the backstop.

"Get the ball!" Chris Lavery screamed at David. "Hurry up!"

David finally got a hold of the ball and threw it back to Chris.

"Come on, Jazz!" Terry screamed as Jazz took a deep breath and stepped back into the batter's box. How did Terry get to third base, Jazz wondered. And then she realized that Terry must have run when David was looking for the ball. And Sarah advanced to second.

Well, she thought, there's only one more pitch to go, and then it'll probably be all over. She'd be soaking in the tub in no time.

This time, she looked at Chris. At this point, what did it matter if he saw what she looked like? She just wanted to go home. "Bend your knees, Jazz!" Breezy screamed from the Parrots' dugout. Jazz crouched down a little and waited. Everyone was always giving her so many instructions. Her legs were killing her. Chris grinned at her and then went into his windup. As soon as she saw the ball, Jazz swung at it.

To her surprise, the bat vibrated as it made contact

with the ball. Jazz had a hard time keeping the bat steady as she followed through on her swing, like Terry had told her to. Jazz just stood and watched as the ball flew over the head of the shortstop and bounced in front of the leftfielder. She couldn't believe it. She had hit the ball! She had actually hit the ball!

Suddenly she heard someone shouting at her. She turned and looked at her dugout.

Ro was standing on the top step, yelling and gesturing wildly with her hands. "Run, Jazz, run!" Ro screamed.

"Go, Jazz! Go to first!" Breezy yelled from the bench.

Jazz turned back toward the field and saw Terry zipping toward her from third base, her brown hair flying behind her. She was yelling something at Jazz, but she couldn't make out what it was.

Suddenly, Jazz realized what was happening. If she didn't hurry up, she was going to be out. She took off for first base as fast as she could. Halfway up the base path, she realized she was still holding the bat. Jazz threw it toward the dugout and slid—by mistake—into first base. As she was lying there in the mud, it occurred to Jazz that one of Ro's big rules was that you never, ever slide into first. Oops, Jazz thought. But still, she'd gotten a hit—her first hit ever. She stood up just in time to see Sarah cross home plate.

The Parrots all ran out onto the field, yelling. Jazz just stood at first, looking around in confusion. What were they all doing? She had gotten a hit. Why were they all out on the field screaming? "We won!" Terry shouted, running over to first base. She grabbed Jazz and lifted her off the ground. "We won! Way to go, Jazz!"

Suddenly, it hit Jazz. They had won! And, *she* had batted in the winning runs! Jazz allowed herself to be dragged over to the rest of her team. She was covered with mud, but she didn't care anymore. She jumped up and down, cheering with the others. She thought baseball was absolutely the greatest thing in the whole world!

2

"Mom!" Jazz screamed, bursting into the Neptune Diner. The rest of the Pink Parrots were right behind her. "Mom, I got a hit!" Jazz's family owned the Neptune Diner, a popular hangout for junior-high and high-school kids in the town of Hampstead, where they all lived.

Mrs. Jaffe came out of the kitchen and smiled at the girls. She looked like an older version of Jazz, right down to the long blonde hair and blue eyes. "That's wonderful, honey," she said, hugging her daughter. "Why don't you girls sit down and Eddie will be right out to take your order." She gave Jazz another hug and walked back into the kitchen, the door swinging behind her.

"We did it!" cheered Kim, throwing her still-wet arm around Breezy's mud-splattered shoulder. They all walked over to two adjoining booths and sat down.

"I told you we were winners!" said Ro, reaching up her hand to give Jazz a high five.

Jazz's father walked in the front door, carrying a box of lettuce. "Hey, gang, game over?" he asked, walking over to the Parrots. "How'd we do?"

"We won!" Jazz announced proudly.

Jazz's little sister, Meg, was right behind Mr. Jaffe. "You did?" she asked happily. Meg, a nine-year-old with a round face, straight, dirty blonde hair and bangs, loved the diner. She was always begging Mr. and Mrs. Jaffe to take her to work with them, even on weekends. Jazz couldn't understand it. She and her older sister, Dana, each had to work at the diner two days a week after school. Jazz hated being in the kitchen peeling potatoes and boring stuff like that. She couldn't wait till she was old enought to waitress like Dana.

"We sure did! And your sister here drove in the winning runs!" said Ro, turning Jazz's baseball cap around on her head, so that the bill was in the back. Jazz knew her hair was probably already hopelessly tangled from the rain, but for once in her life, she didn't care. Hitting that ball was one of the most incredible experiences. She had had no idea that hitting was so . . . so . . . fun!

Ro went straight to the jukebox to put on her favorite song, "Lucky Star," an old Madonna tune. Clapping her hands and moving her hips to the beat, she danced back towards their booths. Jazz loved to watch Ro dance. She had great rhythm.

Meg took out a pad and pencil from her apron pocket. Meg hardly ever took her apron off, even at home. "May I take your order, please?" Meg asked, trying not to giggle.

"Hi, squirt," Breezy greeted her. She held out her

hand for Meg to give her a low five. Meg loved Breezy to pieces. Jazz didn't mind because it meant that Meg followed Breezy, and not her, around all the time.

"Hi, Breeze! What do you want to have?" she asked, holding her pencil above her pad.

Jazz knew better than to let Meg write down everyone's orders. It always took forever. "Just tell Mom we want some burgers," she said to her sister.

Meg frowned.

"And I'll have a banana-strawberry milkshake," announced Terry. Terry loved the Neptune's milkshakes. She never left the diner without having one.

"Make mine chocolate," Breezy added quickly.

Meg smiled. Jazz thought she seemed happy to have something to write down. She felt bad for not letting her sister take their orders so Jazz ordered a vanilla milkshake. Then, almost all the other Parrots ordered milkshakes or ice cream sodas, too. Meg practically skipped back to the kitchen. Jazz was right, though. It took her sister forever to write everything down.

Breezy leaned back in the booth and tipped back her baseball cap. "Whew," she said, "what a game. For a while there, I thought we might lose that one."

"Yeah, Ten Pin is a tough team to beat," Kim agreed.

"I never doubted you guys for a minute," said Ro, opening up her compact and checking her damp, but still perfect hair. She gave it a couple of pats, which did nothing to reduce its pouffiness. Jazz had once touched Ro's hair and it had felt almost crunchy, probably because of all the mousse and hairspray and stuff she used to keep it so "big," Jazz figured.

"Ten Pin Bowling does have some very good players," Crystal pointed out.

Terry grunted in agreement. "Chris Lavery is a really good reliever, that's for sure."

"Yeah," Kim added. "He was pretty awesome."

"Yeah," Jazz agreed, at the thought of the good-looking pitcher. "Chris is definitely cute. But did you see David Tabb? I can't believe he wears that totally queer black strap around his head to keep his glasses on."

"Jazz, what are you talking about?" Breezy sighed. "We weren't talking about the way they *looked*. We were talking about the way they played," she pointed out to her cousin.

Jazz shrugged. "Sor-ry!" she said sarcastically. Breezy was always saying things like that to make her feel stupid. Jazz's best friend Lindsay would understand what she was talking about. "Well, it's just that you had to notice him," she continued, trying again. "I mean, he was such a geek!" She giggled.

"Listen, Jazz," Terry suddenly said through clenched teeth, "I think it's really spineless to talk behind someone's back like that. I mean, if you have to say something nasty about someone, you should at least have the guts to say it to his face!" She gave Jazz a modified version of her monster look.

Jazz was shocked. What was Terry talking about? She hadn't said anything bad. After all, she and Lindsay and all their friends always talked about other people all the time. They called it "dissing." It was fun. Didn't everybody do it? Why was Terry making such a big deal about it? Jazz looked around then, and saw her mother sliding their plates onto the counter.

"There are the burgers," Jazz said, happy to change the subject. "I'll get them." She jumped up and practically raced to the counter.

The door to the kitchen swung open again, and Eddie Andrews walked out. He was carrying a huge tray with all of their milkshakes on it. Eddie was the only thing about working in the diner that Jazz liked. He worked there in the afternoons and on weekends. His classes at the community college were in the morning and he was studying to be a police officer. He had curly black hair and the most beautiful hazel eyes Jazz had ever seen.

"Hey!" Eddie yelled out, when he saw the crowd of girls in muddy baseball uniforms gathered at the two booths. "Don't tell me—this has got to be a victory celebration. Nobody but a winner could be as wet and dirty as you guys are and still be smiling."

"Hi, Eddie," Jazz said, smiling at him. She walked back to the booths with a few plates. "You're right, we won! It was totally incredible." What Terry had said to her flew right out of her head and all she could remember was that they had won their game.

Eddie put the tray down at the first booth and started handing out the glasses. "Nice going!" he said, congratulating them. "So that makes you, what? Tied for second place in the league, right?" Eddie was a big fan of the Pink Parrots. He wasn't able to go to very many of their games because he was always working or at school.

But he kept track of their wins and losses.

When the tray was empty, Eddie sat down next to Jazz. "So," he said. "Tell me everything. All the details. What was the final score?"

"It was really intense," said Breezy, her dark eyes flashing. "We were losing 6-5 in the last inning—"

"And it was pouring," Kim interrupted, unwrapping her straw and blowing the wrapper at Breezy.

"Cut it out!" Breezy yelled at her. Jazz giggled. The two of them were always bickering about something or other. But they had been best friends as long as Jazz could remember.

"We figured we were sunk," Terry said, taking a gulp out of her shake without even bothering with a straw. Sometimes Jazz got a little embarrassed to eat with Terry. She ate so fast—and so much! And she never closed her mouth when she chewed.

"But we did have last licks," Crystal pointed out. Jazz was shocked to see Crystal actually drinking a root beer float. She always had a salad and water. Crystal was a ballet dancer and she was usually watching her weight.

"Yeah," said Breezy. "So there we were, bases loaded, down by two runs, with one out. And there I am, pacing back and forth in the dugout, just wishing I were up so I could do something . . ."

"And then slugger, here—" Ro said, cutting Breezy off and jerking her thumb towards Jazz, "Comes up. And with two strikes against her, she gets her first hit!"

Eddie smiled at Ro and his face turned red. Jazz was convinced that Eddie secretly had a major crush on Ro.

She could tell because he was always blushing whenever he made eye contact with her. But then Eddie raised his eyebrows and looked at Jazz. "This one, here?" he joked. "Little Goldilocks got a hit?"

Jazz nodded, smiling broadly. Eddie was always teasing her, calling her Cinderella or Goldilocks. She stood up. "It was easy," she said, bragging a little. "I just looked for the ball, and when I saw it coming toward me, I hit it."

"She was great," said Ro. "You should have seen her."

Jazz smiled and blushed proudly.

"Really, Jazz, it's true. You saved the game," Crystal said, turning toward her.

"Even if you did slide into first," Breezy added, laughing.

"That's right," Jazz agreed with a giggle. "I guess I kind of forgot. What's the rule about sliding again, Ro?"

"Always to run through first and never to slide," Ro answered with a smile.

"For a minute I was afraid you weren't even going to run to first," Terry said and laughed.

"I know," Jazz remembered. "I couldn't believe I had really hit the ball. Then I heard Ro yelling and saw you running toward me from third base yelling something, and it all sank in. I probably wouldn't even have run if it weren't for you, Terry. So, in a way, it was probably you who saved the game."

All the Parrots laughed, and Terry just shrugged.

"Really, Jazz, that was great. Chris Lavery was throwing some pretty tricky pitches," Kim said, slurping up some of her strawberry milkshake.

"Yeah," Breezy agreed, suddenly standing up. "He's got this weird delivery. It kind of catches you by surprise." She went into a windup in her best imitation of Chris Lavery.

"Go on, Jazz, you can hit this guy!" Terry exclaimed quickly, pointing at Breezy.

"Let's see the swing that saved the game!" Eddie demanded. "I was stuck at the library and I want an instant replay."

"Let's view the video!" Ro said in a great imitation of Janey Lowry, a local T.V. sportscaster. "And it is Jazz Jaffe up at bat. The game depends on this one pitch, folks, but Jaffe's a good bet. She settles into the batter's box and eyes the pitcher . . ."

Jazz planted her feet on the linoleum tile floor and pretended to lift the bat to her shoulder.

Ro continued the play-by-play. "And the pitcher goes into his windup. He delivers, and it's a fastball straight up the middle."

Breezy went into an exaggerated version of Chris's windup and pitched an imaginary ball to Jazz.

"Jaffe swings, and connects!" Ro cried.

Jazz swung her imaginary bat as hard as she could.

"And it looks like a blooper to leftfield," Ro went on. "Jaffe's on her way to first. The crowd is on its feet."

This time, Jazz remembered what to do right away. She flew by Breezy toward the door to the diner, and got ready to slide just the way she had before, even if she wasn't really supposed to. But it was a play-by-play, and

Eddie had wanted to see what she had really done.

But just as she dropped into her slide, the door to the diner opened. Before she knew what had happened, Jazz had smashed right into a crowd of people and was lying on the floor in front of them.

Jazz looked up from the floor in surprise. Directly above her was Lindsay Cunningham. Lindsay was looking down at her with a shocked expression on her face.

"Um, hi, Lindsay," Jazz said, looking up and smiling. "I was just doing my winning slide."

Jazz stood up, wiping her hands on her dirty baseball pants, and laughed. Beth Douglas, Molly Cooper and Gwen Billings, Lindsay's loyal followers, were right behind Lindsay, and they were all staring at her. Suddenly, Jazz became self-conscious about her muddy uniform, messy hair and dirt-streaked face.

Lindsay looked terrific, as usual, in a denim miniskirt, pale pink sweater, white socks and pink sneakers.

"Hey, Jazz," Sean Dunphy suddenly said as he walked in with Joey Carpenter, Lindsay's boyfriend. "I heard you got the hit that won the game." Sean played for Dew Drop Inn and Joey played on Breezy and Kim's old team, Mitchell Lumber.

Jazz blushed and shifted from one foot to the other. She was about to say it had been no big deal when she noticed Mike Boxer standing next to Sean. Mike was a new kid in their class who Jazz thought was totally gorgeous because he looked like Tom Cruise. She gulped when she spotted him.

"So you won a game. Big deal," Joey commented

obnoxiously. "You girls were just lucky."

"Let's go sit down," Lindsay interrupted, turning to the crowd behind her, and flipping her white-blonde hair over her shoulder. "I mean some of the Pink Parrots' 'dirt' might rub off," she continued, wrinkling her perfect snub nose in disgust and turning her back on Jazz, who was just about to follow them.

Jazz just stood there for a minute watching Lindsay walk away. She looked over to where the Parrots were sitting. They *were* kind of dirty—Lindsay was right. Kim had a big smear of dirt across one cheek, and Crystal's uniform was soaked through. Breezy and Eddie were laughing and playing catch with a little packet of sugar. Terry was taking a huge bite out of a double cheeseburger with everything on it, and pickles and ketchup were sliding out of the side.

She looked down at her own muddy uniform. She was *so* embarrassed that Mike Boxer had seen her looking so disgusting. Maybe if she pulled her hair back and put on some lip gloss she'd go over and try to make a better second impression on him. Magazines were always talking about how important second impressions were as far as guys were concerned.

Jazz ran over to the Pink Parrots' tables and asked if anyone had a hair elastic. Sarah handed her a neon yellow one. "What are you fixing your hair for?" Sarah wanted to know. "We all look pretty gross, but it's not like it matters."

"Really," echoed Terry. "I love being disgustingly dirty. It always gets my mother mad."

Jazz just shrugged and pulled her pale pink lip gloss out of her pocket and quickly put some on her lips. "So who's the lucky guy, Jazz?" Eddie asked suddenly as he came by their table.

"Ed-die," Jazz whined. "Sto-op."

"So where are you going, Jazz?" Breezy wanted to know.

All of the Parrots were looking at Jazz and suddenly she felt kind of funny about the whole thing. Sometimes they were so not cool about stuff like that. "I'm . . . uh . . . just . . . uh . . . going to talk to Lindsay," Jazz finally said.

The other girls just looked at her. Jazz knew that the Parrots didn't exactly like Lindsay and her crowd, but that didn't mean Jazz couldn't be friends with them.

Jazz walked quickly over to Lindsay's table, her heart beating just thinking about adorable Mike Boxer. Jazz had written his name 20 times already in her notebook. Lindsay, who was eating chocolate ice cream and laughing at something Mike had just said, looked up as soon as Jazz got to the table.

"Hey, Jazz," Sean said. "I can't wait till we play you guys. We're going to whip you."

Jazz just giggled and went to pull over a chair. Just as she was about to sit down she noticed that everyone was staring at her—especially Lindsay. "Jazz," Lindsay finally said, "don't you think you should, like, clean up or something?"

Beth, Molly and Gwen started to giggle.

"Yeah," echoed Joey. "Go back to your stupid team."

Lindsay laughed, and Sean and Mike didn't say any-thing—they just looked at her. Jazz pushed back her chair and stood up. "Bye," Jazz mumbled, her face flushed with embarrassment.

Jazz felt really stupid. How was it that she was always saying and doing the wrong thing, and why hadn't Lindsay even stuck up for her? She heard loud laughter just then and looked up. Terry had Kim on her shoulders and was busy bumping into Crystal who had Breezy on her shoulders. They all looked like they were having a lot of fun. Why wasn't Jazz having fun? She felt as though she didn't fit into anybody's group anymore.

3

On Monday morning, Jazz rushed down the hall toward the science lab. She couldn't imagine how it had gotten so late. She had just stopped for a minute in the bathroom on the second floor to reapply her Charming Cherry lip gloss. Now, if she didn't hurry, she was going to be late for class.

It was a good thing she had science, instead of some other subject. Mr. Krasdale, the science teacher, was late to class himself half of the time. With his long white lab coat, wild frizzy black hair and black-rimmed glasses, he was just like a typical nutty professor in an old movie. He was always rushing around talking to himself, and sometimes he even forgot when or where the class met. Jazz knew that if she could just get there ahead of him, she'd be all right.

Jazz hurried down the hall, clutching her books, her blonde hair flying behind her. She slid around the corner and pulled open the door to the science lab, practically falling into the room.

What luck, she thought. The kids were all there, but the class hadn't begun yet. Mr. Krasdale was probably wandering through the halls somewhere.

Jazz slid into the empty seat next to Lindsay with a sigh.

Lindsay turned her head toward Jazz and gazed at her coolly with her hazel eyes. Lindsay was wearing a pink and white striped mini-dress and white strappy sandals. She had a pink bow on her white-blonde ponytail.

"Sorry," Lindsay said, "but someone's already sitting there."

Jazz stared at her in surprise. "Lindsay, what do you mean?" she asked. "I always sit with you in science."

"Not *always*," Lindsay contradicted, tightening her bow. "Today someone else happens to be sitting in that seat."

Jazz looked around. Lindsay was right. Someone else was sitting there. There an open notebook on the table in front of her. Who could it be? Just then she saw Gwen Billings heading toward her from the pencil-sharpener.

Gwen stood in front of Jazz and put her hands on her hips. "I think you're in my seat," she said nastily, tossing her brown curls off her shoulders.

Jazz felt her face begin to burn. How could Lindsay not have saved a seat for her? They *always* sat together in science. But there was Gwen, standing above her, waiting for her to move.

As quickly as she could, Jazz slid out of the chair and headed straight for the next empty seat she saw. As soon as she sat down, she opened up her science book and pretended to be very interested in reading about earthworms. She started blinking very fast so she wouldn't cry. The last thing she wanted was for Lindsay and Gwen to see that she was upset.

Jazz couldn't figure it out. Why hadn't Lindsay saved a seat for her? It couldn't have anything to do with what had happened at the diner on Saturday, could it?

"So," Peter Tolhurst suddenly said, interrupting Jazz's thoughts. She looked up from her science book. Peter grinned at her from the seat next to her. She hadn't even noticed he was there. "That was some game on Saturday."

"Oh, hi, Peter," she said, taking a deep breath. She was relieved to have Peter to sit next to. He was a really sweet guy and so nice. Jazz thought he was kind of cute, with his dark brown hair that curled over the collar of his T-shirt. Plus, Peter was really popular with everyone in the school. He was a great athlete. "You were at that game?" Jazz asked in surprise. She didn't remember seeing him or anyone else there.

"Uh, sure," Peter stuttered. "I, uh, I didn't have anything else to do until my game at four, so I, uh, watched yours." He blushed and looked down at the table in front of them. Peter got very busy all of a sudden looking for a pen.

"In the rain?" she asked, her blue eyes widening in shock. Why in the world would Peter sit for hours watching a baseball game in the rain? It sounded pretty ridiculous to her.

"It wasn't that bad, Jazz," Peter replied, grinning. "It was only drizzling." He paused and his green eyes kind of lit up. "Breezy pitched a great game, didn't she? She only allowed two earned runs."

Jazz stared at him. Kim was right. Peter Tolhurst had a crush on Breezy. Jazz giggled at the thought of Peter and Breezy going on a date—they just weren't exactly the dating types. Breezy would probably punch him if he wanted to hold her hand or something. Just then the door opened. Mr. Krasdale walked in muttering to himself, as usual.

"Here comes Dr. Frankenstein," Peter whispered to Jazz. He grinned and nodded in the direction of the teacher. Mr. Krasdale's hair was sticking straight out on both sides of his head.

Jazz giggled. Mr. Krasdale was totally weird. Jazz sometimes thought he was secretly building a monster after school in the science lab.

Jazz spent most of the class drawing little Frankenstein monster heads in the margin of her notebook, and almost forgot about Lindsay and how she wouldn't let her sit with her.

Lindsay ignored Jazz for the rest of the day and all day Tuesday. Jazz had no clue what the problem was. She had tried to sit with Lindsay at lunch on Tuesday, after eating with the Pink Parrots the day before. Lindsay had slid over on the bench, filling up the only space left and said something about how it was just too crowded. Jazz had ended up eating with Terry.

That afternoon after school, Jazz made a special effort

to get to the Neptune on time. Working at the diner on Tuesdays and Thursdays had kept her busy enough. But now, with baseball practice added on Wednesdays, it seemed like she was always hurrying off somewhere after school.

She was rushing down the hall on her way to her locker. Suddenly, she saw Lindsay standing with Molly, Beth and Gwen by a bank of lockers. The four girls were whispering and giggling. They were definitely dissing about someone, and Jazz thought it looked like something really juicy. She wondered who they were talking about and what they were saying.

Jazz hurried over to them, anxious to join the conversation. But as soon as she got there, Beth looked up at her and stopped talking. Then she nudged Lindsay with her elbow, and all four of them suddenly became very quiet.

"Hi, guys," Jazz said, trying to pretend that she didn't notice. "What's up?"

"Oh, nothing," Lindsay replied airily. She looked at the other three girls. "Actually, we were just getting ready to go, weren't we?"

Molly nodded. "That's right," she agreed. "We really have to go somewhere."

"Oh," Jazz said blankly. "Well, I have to work this afternoon at the Neptune. Why don't you guys stop in there later on for an ice cream or something?"

"Well, maybe," Lindsay said glancing at Beth, Molly and Gwen. "But we probably won't have time."

"That's right," Beth agreed. "We might be kind of busy."

"Yeah," Molly echoed. "Busy."

"Oh," Jazz said, confused. She wondered what they could all be doing without her that was so important. She tried to smile. "Well, come by if you have time, then. O.K.?"

But the four other girls had already turned and were on their way down the hall before Jazz finished her sentence. She fought the urge to follow them and ask them where they were going.

Jazz tried to forget about it, but she had a queasy feeling in her stomach the entire afternoon. She couldn't understand why Lindsay had been acting so mean lately. She refused to believe that it was because of her muddy, wet uniform on Saturday. True, she had slid into them. And more than anything else, Lindsay hated to be embarrassed. But that couldn't be it. Jazz knew there had to be something more to it. After all, Lindsay *was* one of her best friends. But what?

She tried to put it out of her mind, but she couldn't fall asleep that night. And the next day in school was no better than Monday or Tuesday. Lindsay and Beth and all the rest of them ignored her or just stopped talking when she tried to say hello. So Jazz ate lunch with Terry again on Wednesday.

Jazz was really pleased when she saw Lindsay walking toward her after school.

"Hi, Jazz," said Lindsay, leaning against Jazz's locker door and smiling sweetly. "Listen, can I ask you a question?"

Jazz smiled back. It was great to have Lindsay talking

to her again. Jazz hated having anyone mad at her. "Sure," she said. "What is it, Linz?"

"Well, remember that dress you had on last week? The pink one, with the bows?" Lindsay asked.

Jazz nodded. She knew right away which dress Lindsay was talking about. It was a very straight cut, sleeveless mini-dress, made out of pale pink cotton, and had a row of little white bows down the back instead of buttons. Jazz had fallen in love with it and had begged for it for her birthday. At first her mother had said it was too expensive. But then Jazz said she was willing to have that be her only birthday present this year. Mrs. Jaffe had given in.

Her mother had put her foot down when it came to wearing the dress to school. Mrs. Jaffe said that it should be saved for special occasions. But Jazz loved the dress so much. She knew she just had to wear it to school once so that everybody could see it. So one day last week she had secretly packed it in her school bag. She had changed clothes in the bathroom early in the morning.

"Well," Lindsay said in her sweetest voice, "didn't you say you got that dress at the mall?"

"Yeah," said Jazz. "My mom got it for me there, at Serendipity." She opened her locker and pulled out her bookbag. She stood there for a minute looking at her books. She really couldn't remember which subjects she had homework in.

Lindsay sighed and shook her head sadly. "I thought that's what you said," she said. "But I went to Serendipity to look for it and I couldn't find it anywhere." Jazz thought her friend looked really depressed.

"Well, I'm sure that's where she got it, Lindsay. I know, because I picked it out." Jazz told her. English and science, the thought struck her. She had homework in English and science. Grabbing her science textbook, Jazz bent down and starting rummaging for her copy of *The Red Pony*. Her locker was pretty messy, she thought.

Lindsay brightened visibly. "Oh, so you could probably find it again!" she said.

"Sure, I only got it a little while ago," Jazz assured her. "They had a bunch of them. They were in this section called 'Ribbons and Buttons,' or something like that." She finally found *The Red Pony* and stuffed it in her school bag.

"That's great," Lindsay said enthusiastically. "Listen, if we went there together, do you think you could find the display again?"

Jazz thought for a moment. Serendipity was by far the biggest store in the mall, but she had gone to look at her dress at least twice before her mother had finally agreed to get it for her. "I know I could find it," she told Lindsay confidently.

"Oh, good," said Lindsay. "Could we go today?"

"Today?" Jazz repeated. "Like right now?"

"Yes, I really have to get the dress right away," Lindsay explained, looking crestfallen. "It's very important."

Jazz didn't even hesitate. Only yesterday, she had been worried that Lindsay might not want to be her friend anymore. And today, here she was, asking Jazz to go to the mall with her as if nothing had happened.

"Sure, I'd love to go," said Jazz, happily stuffing the last of her books into her flowered canvas shoulder bag. She shut her locker and the two girls walked out of the school together.

By the time they got to the mall, Jazz's stomach was rumbling. "I'm starved," she said, turning to Lindsay. "Do you want to go to the Dairy Barn and get an ice cream first?"

"Well, O.K.," Lindsay replied slowly. "I'm hungry, too. But then let's go right to Serendipity afterwards."

At the Dairy Barn, Lindsay gave her order to a man in a white hat behind the counter. "I'll have a single scoop of pralines 'n' cream, please."

Jazz had been dreaming about a double-scoop hot fudge sundae with nuts and whipped cream. She was opening her mouth to give her order, when she heard Lindsay squeal.

"Mike! Hi, what are you doing here?" Lindsay practically yelled.

Jazz turned around and saw Mike Boxer standing behind them. He looked totally incredible in his white T-shirt with a surfing logo and a pair of really well-worn jeans. His high-top sneakers were unlaced and he had a pair of sunglasses hanging around his neck. Jazz thought he looked very California.

"Oh, you know," Mike said, shoving his hands in his jean pockets and looking around. "Just hanging out, I guess."

"What's it going to be, miss?" the man behind the

counter asked Jazz impatiently, his ice-cream scoop clenched in his hand.

Jazz suddenly thought that the double-scoop sundae with the works seemed like a totally messy and piggish thing to order. And, after Mike had seen her lying on the floor of the diner in her muddy baseball uniform on Saturday afternoon, the last thing she wanted now was to have him watch her eat a huge mountain of ice cream.

"Um, I'll have the same thing she got," Jazz finally said, pointing at Lindsay's cone.

"Another pralines 'n' cream, coming up," the man said, digging into the bucket of ice cream. He scooped up a single spoonful, dropped it into a cone and handed it to Jazz. She tried not to look disappointed. A single cone did not measure up to a big sundae, though, no matter how you looked at it.

"Mmmm," Mike said. "What am I going to have?" He squinted at the menu board behind the counter. "Give me a double-scoop brownie sundae with extra hot fudge and marshmallow, please."

"Nuts and whipped cream on that?" the man asked.

"Definitely," said Mike, grinning. "And a cherry," he added.

Jazz suddenly wanted what Mike had ordered. She realized that she had never even tasted pralines 'n' cream ice cream before and didn't even know if she'd like it. She took a small lick from her cone.

It's O.K., she thought, looking longingly at Mike's sundae, but it's not hot fudge with whipped cream and nuts.

"Well, I'll see you guys later," said Mike, shoveling spoonfuls of ice cream into his mouth. "I told Joey and Sean I'd meet them over at The Goal Post."

When Mike left, Jazz turned to Lindsay. "Don't you want to go to The Goal Post?" she asked. "Mike said Joey's going to be over there." The Goal Post was a popular sporting goods store in the mall.

Lindsay made a face. "Forget it!" she said. "They're just going to be looking at a lot of footballs and punching bags and boring stuff like that. Why would any girl want to go there? Besides, we have to go find my dress."

The girls walked through the mall licking their cones. Jazz had been to The Goal Post once, but she would never tell Lindsay that. Breezy had taken her there to help her pick out a glove when she had first joined the Pink Parrots. Jazz stopped suddenly in her tracks, remembering something.

"What is it?" Lindsay asked. "What's wrong?"

"Lindsay," Jazz said slowly, thinking, "What day is today?"

Lindsay laughed. "What do you mean what day is it? It's Wednesday, silly. You know, it comes right after Tuesday and right before Thursday?"

Oh no, thought Jazz. Wednesday! She had been so excited about going to the mall with Lindsay, she had completely forgotten about baseball practice.

"Why?" asked Lindsay. "Were you supposed to do something today?"

Jazz opened her mouth, but then closed it. She didn't want Lindsay to think she didn't want to be there with her. Besides, it was too late. She had already missed most of the practice, and there was nothing she could do about it now.

"No, nothing important," she said, popping the end of her cone into her mouth and chewing it. "Oh, here's Serendipity! Let's go find the dress."

Twenty minutes later, the girls were standing in Serendipity, surrounded by fringed vests and cowboy hats.

Lindsay put her hands on her hips. "I thought you said you could find it again," she said, scowling.

Jazz looked around helplessly. "I don't understand it," she said, practically wailing. "I'm sure it was here."

Lindsay sighed. "Well, we've looked everywhere," she whined. The two girls had combed through rack after rack of dresses in every shade of pink, but they had not been able to find Jazz's pale pink one with the bows down the back anywhere.

"Look," Jazz said, pointing to a woman who was standing on a ladder, straightening a stack of jeans on a high shelf. "She looks like she works here. Let's go ask her."

They walked over to the woman. "Excuse me," Jazz began. "Do you know where the section 'Bows and Ribbons' is?"

The woman looked down from her ladder, thinking. "Oh, I know what you're talking about!" she said after a moment.

"You do?" Lindsay cried happily. "Great."

"Yes, yes. 'Buttons and Bows,' it was called," the

woman continued.

"Was?!" Jazz and Lindsay exclaimed together.

"Why, yes, certainly," said the woman, nodding. "It was right here, one of our temporary displays—like this one 'Home on the Range.'" She swept her arm out at all the Western clothing hanging around them.

"Well, what happened to all the clothes that were here before?" Jazz asked, hesitantly. She didn't think she wanted to know the answer.

"We have to find a certain dress," Lindsay told her.

"Well, I don't know," the saleswoman admitted. "Sometimes we move them to another area. What does this dress look like?"

"It's pink," Jazz began.

"And it's got all these little white bows down the back," Lindsay added.

"Oh, I know just the dress you mean," the woman said. "That one was very popular. It sold out almost right away."

"Sold out?!" Lindsay cried.

"That's right," said the woman. "But we should be getting some more in a couple of weeks. Just check back."

"Oh, good," said Jazz, relieved. "Thank you." She turned to Lindsay. "See, Linz, they're getting more. If you want, I'll come back with you when they have it."

Lindsay sighed deeply. Jazz couldn't believe how upset her friend looked. "You don't understand," she said. "I have to have it this week. Before Saturday."

"What's so important about Saturday?" Jazz asked, confused.

Lindsay looked at her. "Oh, Jazz," she said. "I guess I forgot to tell you. I'm having a big roller skating party at Rockin' Rollers on Saturday, and I was thinking of wearing that dress. You're invited, by the way."

"That sounds great, Lindsay!" Jazz exclaimed quickly. "I'd love to come." She couldn't understand why Lindsay would want to wear a dress like that to go roller skating, but Lindsay was very into making sure she looked totally perfect all the time.

"Everybody'll be there," Lindsay continued with a toss of her white-blonde hair. "Joey, of course. And Beth, Molly, Sean, Gwen, and Mike—all the cool kids."

As soon as Lindsay mentioned Mike, Jazz's heart began to beat faster. This was perfect, she thought, a real boy-girl party at a roller skating rink, and she and Mike would both be there.

"The only problem is, I had really been planning on wearing that dress," Lindsay said, pouting. "Now I don't know what to do! I wish I had gotten one earlier, like you did." She looked at Jazz. "It was just that you were so sure that they still had them."

Jazz didn't know what to say. She hated to see Lindsay looking so upset even if it didn't really make sense to her. Somehow she felt responsible, though. She didn't know what to do. Should she lend Lindsay her new favorite dress so she would be happy again? Jazz had already worn it to school once and she wasn't planning on wearing it on Saturday, so maybe it was the right thing to do. It was only a dress, after all. As long as Lindsay didn't mess it up or anything.

"Hey!" Jazz said suddenly. "I have an idea. You can borrow my dress for the party."

Lindsay turned quickly to look at her, a big smile on her face. "Oh, Jazz, could I really?" she said happily.

"Sure," said Jazz, relieved to see Lindsay smiling. "We're about the same size. I'm sure it'll fit you."

Lindsay grabbed Jazz's arm with her two hands. "Oh, thanks, Jazz," she said. "You're the best."

Jazz smiled. It was great to have Lindsay back as a friend. After another hour browsing through some of the stores, the two girls left the mall and walked out into the bright sunshine. "I'm so excited about Saturday," Lindsay said, her hazel eyes twinkling. "I can't wait. We rented a special party room at Rockin' Rollers for the food and drinks and stuff. And I just know Joey's going to love me in that dress. He says I look really cute in anything with a bow. And he says pink is definitely my best color."

Jazz nodded. She was beginning to wonder what *she* should wear to the party.

"Guys really like that kind of stuff, you know," Lindsay confided. "Bows, flowers, lace. It's the best way to get a guy to notice you."

"Do you really think so?" Jazz asked, looking at Lindsay. She definitely wanted to be noticed by Mike Boxer at the party on Saturday.

"Of course," Lindsay said. "Joey says that guys like girls who look like girls." She stopped and turned to face Jazz. "Joey also says that guys like girls who *act* like girls," she added.

41

"What do you mean?" Jazz asked. Sometimes Lindsay said the weirdest things.

"Think about it," Lindsay said, starting to walk again. "If a guy wants to hang out with someone who wears dirty clothes and acts all rough and stuff, he can just hang out with another guy."

"Yeah," Jazz agreed, running a little to catch up to her friend. "I guess that makes sense."

"Which is why guys definitely don't like girls who play sports," Lindsay went on. "Joey says that any girl who plays sports just wants to be a guy. Personally, I can't imagine why any girl would want to spend all day running around on a hot, dusty field. It's so much nicer to just sit in the bleachers with a cold soda and cheer for the guys. Besides, the guys love it. Joey says he always plays much better when I'm there cheering him on."

"Do you really think all guys feel that way?" Jazz asked her, thinking of Mike Boxer, who was friends with Joey, and really wanting to know.

Lindsay tossed her hair. "I'm positive," she said firmly. "Which is why you should quit that dorky baseball team already and start acting like one of my friends again."

"I *am* one of your friends," Jazz protested. "Besides, I don't know. I mean, if I quit the team they'd have to find somebody else to take my place. They only have nine girls, after all."

"So what?" Lindsay replied with a shrug.

Suddenly there was the sound of screeching bike brakes behind them. Jazz and Lindsay whipped around.

It was Breezy on the bike and Jazz thought she looked tired. She was still wearing her sweats, and she was dusty from head to toe. A pair of cleats dangled from the handlebars. Breezy took off her hat and mopped the sweat from her forehead.

"Jazz!" she practically yelled. "Where were you? You were supposed to be at practice!"

Jazz tried to think of something to say. She opened her mouth, but Lindsay cut her off. "What business is it of yours?" she said to Breezy. "She was with me."

Jazz saw her cousin's dark eyes growing even darker, so she jumped in and tried to explain.

"Breezy, I . . . uh . . ." she stuttered. Jazz hated having her cousin mad at her.

But Breezy interrupted her. "Yeah, well, wherever you were, you really missed a killer practice," she said angrily. "Ro had everyone running all over the place. Everyone but you, that is."

"Breezy, I—" Jazz tried again.

But Jazz knew Breezy was really angry. Breezy's eyes were almost black. She practically spat out her words: "Well, I guess we know better than to count on you from now on!"

Lindsay took a step toward Breezy's bike. "So what if Jazz didn't feel like running around with you jerks and getting all disgusting," she hissed.

"Lindsay, why don't you just keep your little powdered nose out of this?" Breezy retorted, turning her bike around.

"Everybody knows that your nose could *use* a little

powder, Breezy—along with the rest of you!" Lindsay replied. "At least I know how to act like a girl! Maybe Jazz felt like acting like a girl, too."

"Looks more like she felt like acting like a loser to me," Breezy muttered, pushing down on her pedal and taking off down the street.

Lindsay looked at Jazz and rolled her eyes. "Can you believe her?" she asked. "What a jerk!"

Jazz bit her lip and sort of nodded. She hadn't even had a chance to say anything to Breezy. Jazz knew the team must have been angry with her for not showing up, but she didn't want Lindsay to think she was defending her cousin.

Lindsay hooked her arm through Jazz's. "Come on," she said, almost gaily. "I have an idea. Let's go straight to your house now, so I can try on the dress. And then, afterwards, we can go over to my house. I just got this really cool curling wand, and we can do each other's hair."

"O.K.," Jazz said, anxious to please Lindsay. Maybe if the curling wand really made her hair look great she'd ask Lindsay if she could borrow it before the party on Saturday.

4

Jazz sat on the bench between Crystal and Breezy, watching Ro pace back and forth. It was Friday, and Ro had called an extra practice session. She said that there were a few things that the team really needed to work on before Saturday's game against Dudley's Bar and Grill.

Ro walked back and forth, snapping her gum. Any minute now she would begin one of her talks. Jazz sneaked a sideways look at Breezy, but Breezy just stared straight ahead of her. Jazz didn't know what to do. Now that Lindsay was talking to her again, Breezy wasn't. In fact, her cousin hadn't said more than two words to her since Wednesday.

Suddenly, Ro stopped pacing and faced the team. She was wearing a pair of white overalls a couple of sizes too big for her, with a wide belt cinching them in at the waist. The belt matched her hot pink T-shirt and high-top sneakers exactly.

"Okay, guys," she began, tightening the pink and white polka-dotted scrunchie holding her high ponytail. "Today I'm going to teach you something about baseball."

Jazz glanced at Crystal on the other side of her. Crystal was sitting up very straight and listening carefully to every word Ro said. Terry, who was sitting next to Crystal, pulled a package of Gummy Bears out of her pocket and popped them into her mouth one at a time. Jazz looked at Breezy again. Her cousin might have been a statue. But Kim, on the other side of her, had trouble keeping still for long. The short, red-haired girl sat on her hands and rocked back and forth.

"Baseball," Ro began, "is like a beauty salon."

Jazz sighed. She thought Ro was great and all, but sometimes she just didn't understand what Ro was talking about.

Jazz looked around and saw that everyone looked as confused as she felt. "Baseball is just like a beauty salon, with a team of people who wash, set, dry, color, cut, style and perm."

Jazz thought of the Pink Parrot Salon, Ro's beauty parlor and the team's sponsor. Jazz loved to get her hair done there. Of course, her mother didn't let her go all that often. If it was up to Jazz, she'd be there every day. Jazz loved all the bottles of nail polish, tubes of special conditioner, exotic shampoos, mousses, gels and other potions that covered every inch of counterspace in the salon. She even liked the smell of hairspray and perm lotion that lingered in the air all the time. There was nothing Jazz loved more than to be fussed over. And Ro made her feel like the most beautiful 12-year-old in the world.

"Check this out, Parrots," Ro continued, interrupting

Jazz's thoughts. "Imagine for a minute that one of the girls in the shop makes an appointment for someone to come in for a wash and set. Now, say that this girl isn't around when her customer arrives. Say she went out and took an extra half-hour for lunch or something. What happens?"

Jazz looked around. She had no idea what would happen. And she had no idea what any of this had to do with the game against Dudley's Bar and Grill the next day.

"Somebody else who works there has to do it?" Kim asked, rocking faster on her hands.

"Right!" Ro exclaimed excitedly. She pointed a long neon pink and white polka-dotted fingernail at Kim. Jazz loved Ro's fingernails. Ro changed the color and design on them practically every day. And she had these cool little diamond chips and charms that she sometimes glued on the tips of her nails. Jazz wanted to grow her nails as long as Ro's, but her mother would never allow that. Anyway, they kept breaking almost every time she put on her glove.

"That's exactly what happens!" Ro continued. "Someone else in the salon has to take care of this girl's customer. So, maybe I say I'll take care of this customer who wants the wash and set. But maybe I'm already doing a trim. So what do I do?"

Jazz thought she knew the answer to this one. She raised her hand excitedly. "I know, Ro, you see if someone else can do the trim for you," she volunteered.

Ro smiled at Jazz. Jazz sat up a little straighter. She

47

loved pleasing Ro. "O.K., fine," she said, nodding at Jazz. "So let's say I ask someone else to finish my trim for me. But maybe the girl I ask to finish my trim for me is already working on a perm. And maybe she does the trim for me. But because she is so busy, maybe she accidentally ends up letting the perm sit too long. And then, by the time she remembers, it's already ruined. So the woman who came in for the perm ends up with hair that looks like she stuck her finger in a light socket!"

Everyone laughed. Jazz knew exactly what Ro was talking about. Once, last year, Beth Douglas had gotten a perm. And she had definitely looked as if she had been electrocuted, her hair was so tightly curled and sticking out from her head every which way.

"Yeah," said Ro, nodding. "It sounds very funny. But when this woman sees her light-socket hair, she starts to scream. And all the other women in there having their hair done look over to see what she is screaming about. When they see this awful perm, they decide that they're never coming back to the salon because they're afraid they'd end up looking that way, too."

Jazz knew that was true, too. Beth had sworn that she would never go back to that place at the mall where she got her perm.

"And they all tell their friends about this," Ro continued, looking Jazz right in the eye. Jazz started squirming under her scrutiny. "Of course, the woman with the hair, she complains to all her friends, too. And before long, we have no business at the salon at all. Eventually, if things keep up that way, it hurts every person who works at the Pink Parrot Salon."

"I think I understand," Crystal said suddenly. "You're talking about teamwork." Jazz stared at her in surprise. What was Crystal talking about? Ro was talking about bad perms. What did curly hair have to do with teamwork?

Ro smiled at Crystal. "Bingo! You got it!" she exclaimed. "In the beauty parlor, if one girl doesn't do her part, the whole group suffers. It's the same in baseball. If one player doesn't give a hundred percent, she can ruin it for the rest of the team."

Jazz bit her lip. Suddenly, she thought she understood what Ro was saying. And it seemed like a lot of it was meant especially for her. She began to feel really sorry about missing practice on Wednesday.

"That's how all the really great teams did it. They weren't just a couple of stars—they pulled together as a team. Look at the Mets in 1969. Look at the Dodgers in 1988."

The only thing Jazz knew about the Mets was that Ron Darling was really cute. But 1969 was before she was born. She was pretty sure that Ron wasn't playing for the Mets then. And she didn't know any of the players on the Dodgers at all.

Ro kept talking, but Jazz stopped paying attention after that. She was thinking that she really didn't have much time to figure out what to wear to the roller skating party. She was sorry about missing practice and all, but she had a lot of other things besides baseball on her mind. If Lindsay was going to dress up for the party, then maybe Jazz should too. She had to make sure she looked just right for Mike Boxer.

"So that's what we're going to work on today," Ro finished, pacing up and down in front of them again. "Teamwork. We're going to remind ourselves that a baseball team is not just nine players. It's one team, working together. Today I'm going to put you in different groups so you can work together."

Ro looked at each girl on the bench. Jazz thought she looked at her the longest. "Crystal, you work with Betsy today over there in leftfield," she instructed. "Kim, you and Julie and Andrea stay here and work on batting." Ro sent Terry and Sarah to centerfield. Finally, she said, "Breezy, why don't you work with Jazz over in rightfield for a while?"

Jazz sighed. She couldn't believe that she had gotten Breezy as her partner. Her cousin was still mad at her for missing practice. Jazz turned and looked at her. Breezy looked about as enthusiastic about the situation as Jazz felt.

"O.K., Jazz," Breezy finally said, standing up. "Let's go." She walked out of the dugout and headed for rightfield. "Come on, Jazz!" Breezy called over her shoulder, irritated. Jazz jumped up and trotted after her cousin.

Breezy told her to stand out in rightfield where she usually did. "I'm going to throw the ball out to you. Field it and throw it back to me at first. O.K.?" Breezy instructed, walking over to somewhere near first base.

Jazz waited for Breezy to get to first. It was a warm

day, with a little wind—her favorite kind of weather. She noticed two guys walking toward the outfield. On days like this, Jazz almost didn't mind being out on the field at all. It would have been better to be lying in the sun. But at least she was *in* the sun. Maybe she'd even be able to get a suntan in time for Lindsay's party. Jazz thought her blonde hair looked so much blonder when her skin was a little darker. She liked the contrast.

Jazz was so busy watching the two guys walking across the outfield that she didn't notice the ground ball that Breezy had whizzed toward her. The ball went right by her and Jazz didn't even see it.

"JAZZ!" Breezy exclaimed impatiently. "Why didn't you get that ball? You weren't even looking!"

Jazz turned toward her cousin. What was Breezy yelling about now? Breezy looked pretty mad. She was practically jumping up and down at first base.

"Pay attention!" Breezy yelled. "I have better things to do with my time!"

Jazz tried to look as if she was paying attention. *She* had better things to do with her time, too. Like get a tan. Or decide what to wear to Lindsay's party.

"O.K., here it comes!" Breezy yelled, as she bounced the ball right toward Jazz. Jazz made an effort to stop it, but the ball still rolled right between her legs.

Breezy looked even more exasperated. "Jazz, you have to stop the ball with your glove," she yelled. Then she shrugged her shoulders. "Here, bounce it toward me. I'll show you."

Jazz ran back for the ball and picked it up. She took a

deep breath of warm air. It was really starting to get hot. She thought it was too bad her baseball cap kept the sun off her face. She turned her cap around so the brim was in the back and raised her face toward the sun.

Suddenly she heard Breezy's voice. *"JAZZ!"* her cousin practically screamed at the top of her lungs. "Bounce me the ball!"

Jazz opened her eyes and turned around. Breezy was standing with her arms folded over her chest. Breezy was never any fun when baseball was concerned, Jazz thought.

Jazz bent down and bounced the ball toward her cousin. It moved slowly along the grass for a few yards, and finally came to a stop long before it got anywhere near where Breezy was standing.

"Ugh!" Breezy exclaimed, running forward to where the ball had stopped.

"Hey, Terry!" Breezy yelled to Terry, who was working with Sarah in centerfield. "Throw me a grounder so I can show Jazz how to field it." She tossed the ball to Terry, who caught it easily in her glove.

Terry then bounced the ball quickly to Breezy, who scooped it up effortlessly in her glove, transferred it to her throwing hand and shot it back to Terry.

"See that?" said Breezy. "Notice how I scooped the ball in front of me while blocking it with my body?"

Jazz nodded. She wasn't really listening, though. The two guys she had seen walking across the field had reappeared. She recognized them as the two high school guys who worked as groundskeepers for the park.

"O.K., Jazz, now you try," Breezy instructed.

Terry bounced the ball out to Jazz. She ran toward the ball with her glove lowered to grab it. Misjudging the speed at which the ball was traveling, Jazz whipped right past it without even making contact with it, let alone catching it.

"Throw it here," Terry called, as Jazz turned around and ran back to get the ball. Jazz picked up the ball and hurled it in the general direction of Terry. It ended up near second base instead.

"Jazz!" Breezy yelled again. "Would you watch where the ball is going? This time keep your eyes glued to what I'm doing. See how I try to look for where the ball is going to go, and then I bend over and just let it roll right into my glove? Roll it at me again, Terry!"

Jazz tried to look at Breezy, but out of the corner of her eye, she noticed that one of the guys had gotten on a lawnmower and started cutting the grass beyond the baseball field.

Breezy continued to demonstrate, but Jazz was finding it harder and harder to concentrate on what Breezy was saying and doing. Jazz's eyes followed the lawnmower as it traveled back and forth across the grass, getting closer and closer to where she was standing.

Finally, it stopped right on the other side of the fence. Jazz noticed that the guy on it had thick wavy brown hair and an incredible tan—probably from working outside.

"Wow, it's the girls playing baseball," he called over the fence. "You girls are my favorite team to watch."

Jazz gave him her best smile and flipped her hair over

her shoulder. Suddenly she heard Breezy calling her name.

"Jazz! Jazz! Are you paying attention? You try it now!" her cousin yelled out.

Breezy bounced her the ball, but Jazz wasn't trying very hard and she missed again. She looked over to where the guy was leaning against the fence, shrugged and smiled.

"Come on, Jazz!" Breezy yelled, practically hoarse. "Are you really concentrating? Watch me do it a few more times. See? You have to bend into the ball in a forward motion." She ran to the ball and picked it up.

As Breezy threw the ball back to Terry, Jazz looked at the guy, who was trying to start his lawnmower again. He tried several times, but it was stalled. Finally, he began kicking it.

The other guy, who was watering the grass a few yards away, saw what was happening and put down his hose. Jazz noticed that he, too, had a deep tan, and that his hair was blond. They were both pretty gorgeous.

Jazz watched as the second guy tried to start the mower and failed. She had completely forgotten about Breezy, who was still fielding the balls that Terry was throwing.

The first guy looked at Jazz and shrugged, smiling.

"What happened?" she called out to him, taking off her baseball cap. Jazz started walking toward the fence.

"Oh, the stupid thing does this all the time," the blond-haired guy said, still looking down at the machine in front of him. "They really need to get a new one."

"But if it had to break down, it picked a great spot for it," the other guy said, grinning up at her.

Jazz smiled back at him and leaned against the fence, ready to start a conversation.

"*JAZZ!!!*" Breezy called loudly. She sounded really mad. Jazz turned to face her cousin quickly.

Breezy was stalking out to where Jazz was standing. Her face was very red and she was swinging her glove violently as she walked.

"What's going on?" Breezy demanded, stopping a few inches away and putting her face right up to Jazz's. "Where are you, on Mars? What are you doing over here? You were supposed to be watching." Her dark eyes were flashing.

Jazz lowered her eyes and shrugged. The lawnmower and the boys were much more interesting than fielding ground balls. Why couldn't Breezy understand that? Lindsay and Beth and their friends would know exactly how she felt—not only were these guys total hunks, they were in high school. Incredible. Now that Breezy was yelling, Jazz could kiss her first impression on the boys good-bye. Breezy was making Jazz sound like a jerk in front of them and that just wasn't fair.

Breezy folded her arms across her chest. When Jazz didn't answer, she yelled, "Forget it! I can't believe I'm even wasting my time with you!"

"No, you forget it," Jazz yelled back at Breezy. "You're the worst teacher ever."

Breezy stormed away, heading for the dugout.

Jazz stood there for a minute trying to calm down.

Breezy was the most difficult person, she thought. And she didn't know how come it was that she kept making her cousin mad. She never meant to—it just happened. And then Breezy would start yelling. Jazz hated to be yelled at. She always tuned out what people said if they were yelling.

"Come on, Jazz, I'll practice with you," Terry said, startling Jazz. Terry had walked over as soon as she had seen Breezy and Jazz start fighting. Jazz hadn't even seen her coming. Looking over at the boys standing by the lawnmower, Terry said, "Don't you guys have grass to cut or something?"

The two hunks weren't even trying to start their motor anymore. They were both totally engrossed in the girls' conversation. They looked as if they were trying hard not to laugh about something. Jazz couldn't imagine what was so funny.

Terry glared at the guys, her arms folded across her chest, giving them a minor version of her monster face.

"They can't start it," Jazz explained to Terry with a giggle. "It's broken."

Terry raised her eyebrows at Jazz. "Let me take a look," she said gruffly, jumping the fence.

Jazz watched as Terry grabbed the starter and gave it a tremendous yank. The lawnmower roared to life immediately. The boys' mouths hung open in astonishment as they looked from the humming mower to Terry and back again. Terry jumped back over the fence and landed beside Jazz. Trying not to laugh, Jazz stared at the guys.

"Come on, Jazz," Terry said, wiping her hands on her

sweats. "We have to get back to practice."

Terry led Jazz to the middle of rightfield. Jazz glanced over her shoulder at the guys. Neither of them had even moved toward the mower. They just stood there. Jazz giggled. Sometimes Terry could be so funny.

"I'm going to give you Terry's Official List of Pointers," Terry began after they had stopped walking. "Now, I want you to memorize all of them, because you're going to be tested on them later."

Jazz sighed. She didn't know if she could remember anything else. Baseball got so confusing sometimes. There were so many things to remember that Jazz wound up forgetting almost all of them most of the time. She couldn't keep anything straight. And now, Terry wanted to test her some more. . . . Jazz did not think that was a good idea at all.

"First of all," Terry began, backing up. "You have to keep your eyes planted firmly in your head at all times."

Jazz giggled. What in the world was Terry talking about? Where else did Terry think she might keep her eyes?

"Now," Terry continued in a stern voice. Jazz noticed that Terry was trying hard not to laugh, though. "Notice how when I throw the ball, my fingers never leave my hand?" Terry went on, smiling. Jazz began to giggle.

"And, of course, how my hand never leaves my wrist?" Terry added. Jazz laughed out loud. There was going to be no problem remembering these things. Practice with Terry was definitely different than with Breezy. Jazz figured this might even be fun.

"Finally, when fielding the ball, remember to keep your knees between your calves and your thighs at all times," Terry instructed.

Jazz was laughing so hard she was crying. She wiped the tears with the back of her glove.

"But most important," said Terry, "is to forget all these rules and all the other ones everybody's always trying to tell you, and just relax and have a good time. Baseball is supposed to be fun!"

Terry backed up and tossed Jazz the ball lightly. Jazz was pleased that she just managed to catch it in the webbing of her glove.

"All right!" Terry complimented her. Jazz smiled broadly. "Now let me have it!"

Jazz threw the ball back. It was a little short, but Terry got it into her glove just before it would have hit the ground.

Next, Terry backed up and threw Jazz a higher, arcing ball. Jazz just put her glove up and the ball landed smack inside it.

"Nice," Terry told her. This time Jazz threw the ball a little harder, and Terry had to reach up to get it.

Terry rolled a grounder to Jazz. When Jazz tried to run toward it the way Breezy had shown her, it slipped between her knees. She looked up, hoping that Terry wouldn't be too mad at her.

"Don't worry about it. Don't even think about it," Terry assured her. "It's no big deal. If you miss it, just run after it and throw it in."

Jazz ran back and grabbed the ball. She smiled at Terry

and tossed it back to her. This wasn't so bad, she thought. It was even kind of fun. She never thought baseball was that much fun before—except, of course, when she got her famous hit. Now that had been fun!

"That throw was much better," Terry called out. "Now, let's try another grounder." She rolled the ball to Jazz again. Jazz ran in toward it. She remembered to get her glove on the ground and keep her body behind the ball. Still, Jazz was totally shocked when the ball rolled right into her glove.

"Nice going, Jazz!" Terry praised her. Jazz smiled proudly. Baseball wasn't even that hard, she thought.

As the practice went on, Jazz realized how much Terry was actually helping her. Because she didn't yell at Jazz when she made mistakes, Jazz began to relax on the field. And the more she relaxed, the easier it was to catch the balls that Terry threw.

After a little while, Terry began throwing some tougher ones. At one point, she whizzed a line drive right at Jazz. Without even thinking, Jazz raised her glove up in front of her to protect herself and jumped back a little. The ball hit the glove and dropped to the ground right in front of Jazz. She bent down, scooped it up and threw it back to Terry.

"Terrific, Jazz!" Ro called out. Jazz had been so busy practicing that she hadn't even noticed when the coach walked out to watch. Ro had been standing there for quite a few minutes. Suddenly, Jazz looked around and realized that the two guys had finished cutting the grass and left. And the sun was much lower in the sky. She didn't know how much time had passed, but it looked like quite a bit now. Usually, Jazz thought the practices were kind of endless. But today's had just zipped by. She wished she could practice with Terry all the time.

Ro turned back to the field and clapped her hands for attention. "All right, everyone! That's enough for today! Let's go over to the bench. I have an announcement."

Following behind Ro, Jazz thanked Terry for helping her.

Terry waved a hand in Jazz's direction. "No problem," she said. "You really started to do O.K. out there."

Jazz smiled. She could tell she had played much better than usual. But she knew she never could have done it without Terry.

Jazz practically collapsed on the bench. Even though it had been fun, she realized all of a sudden that she was exhausted. The other Parrots looked pretty tired, too.

"O.K.," Ro began as soon as everyone had sat down. "As you all know, we have a big game tomorrow against Dudley's Bar and Grill. Now, they are *tough*. They've got some very good hitters. But from what I've seen out here today, there's no doubt in my mind that we can beat them."

The team began to cheer. For once, Jazz joined in the cheering and she was as loud as everyone else.

Ro waited for them to quiet down. "And here's my announcement. Tomorrow, after we 'grill' Dudley's Bar and Grill . . ." she trailed off, waiting for everyone to get the joke. "After we grill Dudley's Bar and Grill, we're going to have a little grill of our own. You're all invited to a barbecue at my place after the game."

An even louder cheer went up from the group on the bench.

"Dudical," Jazz said excitedly to Terry, who was sitting next to her.

"Yeah," Terry agreed enthusiastically. "I love barbecues. I hope she has chicken *and* burgers!"

Jazz sighed happily. She was excited about the barbecue, and she knew she had done well in practice. And Terry was great. Jazz really hoped that they would win the game against Dudley's Bar and Grill the next day. Maybe she would even get another hit. The team would really be in a great mood for the barbecue then.

5

Jazz opened her eyes and stretched, wiggling her toes under the covers. Slowly, she sat up and looked around the room that she shared with her little sister, Meg. Meg's bed was empty. She always got up early, even on weekends. But Jazz loved to sleep late. She couldn't wait until her older sister, Dana, went off to college. Then Jazz would finally have her own room. But that was still three years away, and it seemed a very long time to wait.

Jazz thought that anyone looking at the bedroom would have been able to tell that it was shared by two very different people. Meg loved dinosaurs. The walls on her side of the room were covered with posters of triceratops and tyrannosaurus rex. On her bed sat about ten stuffed dinosaurs. Meg insisted on sleeping with all of them every night. Jazz couldn't figure out how Meg could even fit in the bed with all those things.

On Jazz's side of the room was a dresser and a set of shelves just like Meg's. But Jazz's shelves held all her nail polishes and the top of her dresser was crowded with packets of bubble bath, bottles of lotion, little tubes of lip gloss and her jewelry box. Tacked up all over the walls around her bed were pictures of models she had cut out from magazines. Jazz loved models. She wanted to become one when she grew up.

Suddenly, Jazz remembered what day it was and jumped out of bed. It was Saturday. Lindsay's big party at Rockin' Rollers was that night! And she still hadn't decided what to wear.

She jumped out of bed and practically ran to the closet that she shared with Meg. She began pulling things out of her side. She just had to find the perfect outfit, the one that would make Mike Boxer notice her. What had Lindsay said? Guys like girls who look like girls—that was it.

The first thing she pulled out was her black and white striped T-shirt dress. Holding it up in front of herself and looking in the mirror, Jazz sighed. She had thought she loved the way the dress looked on her, but somehow now it just didn't seem frilly enough. All of a sudden, the stripes began to remind her of a referee's uniform. She had to find something with lace, bows or flowers on it.

She threw it on the bed and pulled out a pale blue cotton dress with three buttons at the neck. This one really brought out the color of her eyes, but it was a little too plain. She needed something prettier, lacier.

Dropping the blue dress on top of the striped one, Jazz looked down and noticed the pale yellow shorty nightgown she was wearing. It was trimmed with two rows of lace on each sleeve and had a little satin bow at the neck. Something like that would be perfect! Jazz shook her head. What was she thinking? She couldn't wear a nightgown to Lindsay's party.

Maybe she should wear pants. She rushed over to her dresser and opened up her pants drawer. She pulled out a few pairs and finally found the ones she was looking for. They were mint green covered with little pink flowers, and cropped at the ankles. Jazz sighed. They were pretty, but she was sure it would be better to wear a dress because Lindsay was.

The pile on the bed was getting bigger, and Jazz still hadn't figured out what to wear. She sat down on top of the dresses on her bed and tried to think. If only she could wear her fancy new pink mini-dress with the bows. But she had lent it to Lindsay. Why didn't she have more things with bows?

Jazz stood up and marched over to the closet, determined to find the right thing to wear. She would just go through everything in the closet. She would only let herself take something out if it had ribbons, bows, lace or flowers on it.

Fifteen minutes later, she sat on the floor, surrounded by clothing. Around her were a purple flowered bathrobe, a long, white lace dress she had worn as the flower girl in her Aunt Bonnie's wedding, a pair of black velvet shoes with white satin bows that she had bought at the mall back in February and never worn and a green velvet tunic covered with blue plastic flowers that Meg had worn as the wood-elf in her school play last year.

She looked around at the pile surrounding her and shook her head. She didn't know what she was going to do with all of this stuff. Somehow nothing seemed quite right. She decided she had no choice but to try and pull something together. First, she dug through the pile on her bed and found the light blue cotton dress that brought out the color of her eyes. She slipped it on and, taking the white lace sash from the flower-girl dress, tied it around her waist. Next, she unpinned a cluster of the blue plastic flowers from Meg's old costume and fastened them on the sash.

Looking at her reflection in the mirror, Jazz sighed. Just then her mother poked her head in the door.

"Morning, sweetie," she said. "You look nice. I'm just heading over to the diner. I'm taking Meg with me." Her eyes traveled past Jazz to the piles of clothes that were all over the room. "Oh, Jasmine, I hope you're going to get all that cleaned up before you leave for the game this afternoon."

Jazz gasped. She had been so excited about Lindsay's party that she had practically forgotten about the game. Well, there was no problem, she figured. She should be back from the game in plenty of time to change and get ready for Lindsay's party.

"O.K., don't worry. I'll put it all away," she told her mother. Mrs. Jaffe waved and closed the door behind her.

Jazz stuffed most of the clothing back into the closet, not really bothering to hang anything up. Jazz stood there for a few more minutes staring at herself in the mirror, and then walked out into the kitchen.

Her sister Dana was sitting at the kitchen table, doing homework. Jazz shook her head. Only Dana would think of doing homework on a sunny Saturday morning. Next to Dana was a box of raspberry-cheese coffeecake, unopened. Jazz picked it up and ripped it open hungrily.

Dana looked up from her books. Her blonde hair was tucked into a neat ponytail, and her glasses had slid part way down her nose.

"Whoa, you're pretty dressed up," she greeted her sister, studying her outfit. "What's this plastic flower action, Jazz? I didn't know you were into that kind of thing. It's not exactly a trendy look, you know."

Jazz tore off a hunk of coffeecake and shrugged, popping it into her mouth. "That's the problem, Dana," Jazz explained with a sigh. "I have no clothes."

Dana watched her chew. "Take human bites. Now tell me what kind of thing you're looking for and maybe I can help," Dana offered, smiling at her sister.

"Well, I'm going to this really really important roller skating party tonight at Rockin' Rollers that Lindsay is having and it's boy-girl and everything and I need something with bows that's frilly to wear because guys like lacy stuff," Jazz blurted out.

"Hmmm," Dana replied. "Bows and frills for roller skating. That sounds kind of strange to me, Jazz. When I think of skating I think of biker shorts and jeans and that kind of look."

"No, Dana, that's not what I want to wear," Jazz explained patiently to her older sister. "I need something really special."

"Well, you could always borrow that pink mini-dress with the white polka-dots and the kickpleats at the bottom that I have," Dana suggested. "I mean, it's kind of too short for me anyway."

"Wow," Jazz gushed. "I would love to, Dana. Can I really?"

"Yeah, yeah," Dana said with a grin.

"You're the best older sister ever," Jazz exclaimed, going over to where Dana was sitting and giving her a big hug. "The best ever."

"Well, I am the only one you've got so I don't exactly have a ton of competition," Dana pointed out sensibly, but Jazz was so excited about the dress she barely heard. "By the way, don't you have a game today?" Dana asked.

Jazz nodded. "Dudley's Bar and Grill," she answered, swallowing another huge mouthful of coffeecake. "We're going to 'grill' them!" She laughed, remembering Ro's joke.

Suddenly, Jazz starting choking on her coffeecake. She had forgotten all about Ro's barbecue. And Lindsay's party was tonight! Why did Lindsay's party and Ro's barbecue have to be on the same night? What was she going to do?

Dana looked worried. "Are you all right?" she asked Jazz, pounding her on the back.

"I'm fine, I'm fine," Jazz answered, finally swallowing. She took a long drink of the orange juice Dana held up and hurried back to her room. She knew she had to figure something out fast.

Jazz sat down on her bed and tried to think. She *had* to go to Ro's barbecue. She didn't want the other Parrots to think she wasn't part of the team. Besides, it sounded as if it was going to be a lot of fun. But she definitely didn't want to miss Lindsay's party. Then she began to get an idea. Why couldn't she go to both? Maybe she could just go to the barbecue for a little while, and then find some way to leave and go straight to the roller rink. That way she'd just be a tiny bit late for Lindsay's party. Anyway, Jazz had read in some magazine that it was good to arrive fashionably late. She just better make sure to be fashionable about the whole thing. That shouldn't be a problem, though, she figured, since Dana was lending her that adorable dress.

But how could she wear that dress to Ro's barbecue? Everyone else would be in shorts and they would know something was up if she showed up dressed like that.

Well, maybe she could change before she went to Lindsay's. But where? Ro's place and Rockin' Rollers were both across town from her house, near the baseball field. It was much too far to come all the way home and change. She would waste too much time.

There was only one answer. She'd have to change at the field. She'd bring a big bag with her clothes for Ro's, but she'd hide another smaller bag in her big bag with her things for Lindsay's party. Then she'd just have to find somewhere at the field to stash the little bag until she could slip out of Ro's and go back to change. Jazz thought it was a pretty good solution.

Meanwhile, she'd better hurry up and pack her things if she was going to make it to the field in time for the game.

She flew into Dana's room and opened her closet. The pink polka-dot dress was right there; Dana was so neat, the complete opposite of Jazz. Jazz held the dress up to herself in front of the mirror and admired it. It was perfect.

By the time she got to the field, most of the Parrots were already warming up.

Terry was still sitting on the bench putting on her catcher's equipment. She grinned when Jazz rushed into the dugout.

"Hey, buddy!" Terry greeted Jazz. "I've been waiting for you. Come on, let's go out there and throw a few before the game starts."

Jazz clutched the plastic bag containing her clothes.

"Uh, O.K., Terry, you go on out, and I'll be there in a minute," she stalled, looking around.

Terry shrugged and walked out onto the field, tossing the ball and catching it in her glove.

Jazz looked around quickly and hurried off to the area behind the bleachers. Slipping the smaller bag holding her party clothes out of the larger bag, she crawled under the bleachers and tucked it into a dark corner. Satisfied that no one walking by would notice the little bag, she skipped back to the bench. She left her shorts and sneakers in the big bag under the bench.

"O.K., Terry, here I come!" she called, hurrying out onto the field.

A few minutes later, the Pink Parrots were assembled on the bench. Ro was pacing back and forth in front of them, getting ready for her first talk of the game.

"O.K., Parrots," she said, stopping in front of them and giving her gum one final crack. "That team over there, they're going to be tough." She nodded her head toward the opposite bench, where the boys from Dudley's Bar and Grill were gathered around their coach. Coach Hoffman was tall and thin and had bright red hair. He was surrounded by players in blue pinstripe uniforms. Jazz thought they looked as if they were having a talk, too.

Ro went on. "They've got some good hitters over there, but we're not going to let that worry us. Because we've got Breezy on the mound, and we've also got some people on this team who have really been working on their fielding." She glanced at Jazz, who felt her cheeks glowing with pride.

"All right," said Ro. "Now, I know I don't have to tell you that this game here is going to be like a barbecue."

"That's right!" Terry exclaimed. "We're going to grill them!"

"Yeah!" Ro exclaimed with a smile. "We're going to light a fire under them!"

"Those guys are toast!" Breezy agreed.

Kim stood up. "They're dead meat!" she added, laughing.

Ro laughed. "That's right!" she said. "Now get out there and cook those guys!"

They all cheered and then ran out onto the field. For the first time, Jazz felt really pumped up for the game. She really thought they were going to win. She was surprised that she was so into it. Plus, she was still kind of nervous about the party/barbecue thing.

It turned out to be a great baseball game—much better

than anyone had expected it to be.

Breezy pitched awesomely, and didn't give up any hits in the three innings she pitched.

Breezy, Crystal and Kim all got hits in the first inning, and a bases-loaded home run by Terry put the Pink Parrots ahead of Dudley's 4-0 right away.

It looked as if the Parrots had the game in the bag until the fifth inning. Dudley's had two runs, with runners on second and third and one out. Julie McKay, who had replaced Breezy after the third inning, was struggling to get Robbie Brooks out with a count of two balls and two strikes.

After fouling off two pitches in a row, Robbie connected. All the way out in rightfield, Jazz heard the sound of the bat hitting the ball and then saw the ball come flying out to her. Almost without thinking, she lined the ball up and got under it. She opened her glove and watched the ball fall right in. Jazz was so shocked that she almost forgot to throw the ball to Sarah at second base. But she didn't forget and the runner was out. As she glanced toward home plate, she saw Terry give her the thumbs-up sign.

"Way to go, Jazz!" Breezy called out from over in centerfield. Jazz turned toward her cousin to see her smiling and waving her glove. She smiled back.

Julie struck out Charlie McGovern on three straight pitches for the third out. Then she retired the side in order in the last inning. The Parrots won the game easily, 4-2.

Twenty minutes later, the girls had changed into their

shorts and sneakers and were lounging in Ro's backyard. They were all reliving the game and drinking sodas. Ro, who was single and lived by herself above the Pink Parrot, had a very big backyard.

"When's the charcoal going to be ready?" Terry asked impatiently, getting up to look at the grill.

"Really!" Kim agreed. "I'm starving!"

Terry poked at the coals with a stick. "They look almost done to me," she stated.

The back door opened and Ro came out, carrying a huge tray. Jazz thought she looked as if she was going to fall over, the way the tray was filled.

"Now, we've got chicken here with my special sauce, and we've got burgers," Ro said, carrying the tray to the picnic table. She unloaded it and wiped her hands on her apron which read, HAIRDRESSERS DO IT WITH STYLE, across the front of it. "You can have whichever you want, or you can have both."

Jazz looked at Terry and saw her smile.

Finally, the coals were ready and they started cooking. Jazz sniffed. It smelled so good. After they had stuffed themselves with chicken, burgers, potato salad, coleslaw and soda, they all lay down on the lawn chairs and grass. Jazz groaned and held her stomach. She had eaten so much that she thought she was going to explode. If she even moved, it would be all over. Then Ro stood up.

"O.K., team," she announced, "it's time to go inside and talk to Pablo! You know how lonely Pablo gets if we leave him by himself for too long." Pablo was Ro's parrot and the team mascot. The girls all moaned. "I can't move!" Kim called out. "I'm too stuffed!"

"Me, too!" Andrea agreed, turning over onto her stomach.

"I'll never eat again," Jazz vowed, moaning even louder. She really hoped that Ro didn't make them all get up.

But she did. All the girls helped her pick up the garbage outside and cart it back in. Ro held the back door open for them. Jazz dropped the pile of paper plates in her hand into the big garbage can near the door and followed everyone inside the salon.

Jazz loved the Pink Parrot. She looked around at the lighted mirrors and the shelves full of creams, powders, lotions, polishes, curlers and makeup. Ro was so lucky to be able to have all this stuff, and to be able to use any of it any time she wanted, Jazz thought. If she didn't become a model, maybe she'd be a hairdresser like Ro. It looked like so much fun.

Ro walked over to the perch where Pablo was sitting. "*Hola*, Pablo! Hello!" she said, stroking the bird's head.

"Come on, Pablo," said Terry, walking over to Ro and the bird. "Aren't you going to say hello to us?"

Pablo dipped his head for a moment. "*¡Ay, caramba!*" he squawked, making the girls all laugh.

"You said it, Pablo," said Ro, holding out a potato chip in front of him. The bird snatched the chip from her hand and swallowed it.

Jazz was looking through the bottles of nail polish

near the manicure table. She had thought her collection at home was impressive, but Ro must have at least twice as many colors here as Jazz had on her shelves.

"Wow, look at all this stuff," Jazz said appreciatively.

"Go ahead, try some," said Ro. "Hey wait, I've got more. Here, let's see."

Ro searched through a couple of cabinets and came out with a box. "Here they are," she said, opening the box and taking out some nail polishes. "Who wants a manicure? Free manicures!" She looked around.

"I've never had a manicure," said Crystal. Crystal lived with her father and two older brothers. Jazz figured that it was probably pretty strange for Crystal, whose mother had died when Crystal was really young, to see so much makeup and stuff around.

Kim walked over to the manicure table next to Jazz and picked up a couple of the bottles of polish. "Look at these wild colors," she said. "Wow, Racy Red."

"Look at this," Crystal pointed out, picking up a bottle. "Forever Fuchsia."

Ro nodded at the girls looking through the bottles of nail polish. "Go ahead," she said. "Pick a color. I'll do your nails."

Crystal put down the bottle she was holding and took a step back. "Oh, no thanks, that's O.K., Ro," she said. "I couldn't."

Ro raised her eyebrows. "Sure you could," she said. "Go on."

"I'll take this one," said Kim, holding up a bottle.

"One manicure, coming up," said Ro, sitting down

74

behind the table and taking one of Kim's hands in hers.

"Now this is really cool!" Terry suddenly exclaimed. She had been wandering around the salon picking up things. Every so often she'd hold something up for Jazz to see. Now she held a plastic tray filled with different colored spray cans.

"Oh, go ahead," Ro told her. "Try some. That stuff is great. And it washes right out."

"What is it?" Jazz asked, putting down the bottle she was holding. This looked even more interesting than nail polish.

Terry held up one of the cans. "It's called Crazy Colors," she said.

Ro looked up from Kim's nails. "It's for your hair," she explained.

"I definitely have to see what I look like with some of this stuff on," said Terry. "Ro, you're sure it washes out, aren't you? My mother would kill me if it turned out that I had to spend the rest of my life with crazy-colored hair." Jazz knew exactly what she meant—her mother would die if Jazz came home with purple hair. Ro was so cool that way—she trusted them to do stuff and treated the Parrots as if they were her friends instead of just a bunch of dumb kids. Jazz thought that was great.

Ro nodded. "Just take one of the robes so you don't get it all over your clothes," she said.

Terry took a robe from a hook on the wall and wrapped it around herself. "Jazz, will you help me spray it on?" she asked.

"Sure," said Jazz excitedly. This sounded as if it was

75

going to be fun. She never guessed that Terry would be into something like this. Jazz thought Terry was only into baseball and heavy metal music.

"What should we do?" Terry asked, rummaging through the tray of cans. "I think I want purple," she said, sitting in one of the big chairs in front of a mirror.

Jazz took the purple spray bottle from Terry. She held it a few inches away from Terry's hair and pushed down on the button. A big blotch of what looked like purple paint appeared on the back of Terry's head. Jazz moved the can up and down, managing to turn the blotch into a stripe that ran all the way down Terry's long, brown hair.

"Are you sure you want it all purple?" Jazz asked doubtfully. It looked so purple and totally unlike any other hair color Jazz had ever seen.

"Yeah, maybe you're right," said Terry. "Let's use some other colors, too. Make me a rainbow."

Jazz giggled as she picked up another can and sprayed a green stripe onto Terry's hair right next to the purple one. Breezy walked over and stood behind Jazz.

"Hey, let me put some on her," Breezy suddenly said. She picked up a can of orange. In no time, Terry looked as if she was wearing a rainbow. Every bit of brown hair was covered by a different color stripe. Jazz thought it looked really wild.

"Well, what do you think?" asked Terry, putting one hand up to her rainbow hair and striking a pose.

"Wild!" said Ro. "I love it!"

"How about my nails?" asked Kim, giggling, as she

walked over to show them her manicure. The color she had chosen was Shocking Pink, and it looked especially shocking on someone with Kim's bright red hair and orange-brown freckles.

"Pink, for the Pink Parrots," she explained with a laugh.

Then Ro got an idea. "Hey, hold on a second," she said, dragging a stool over to a cupboard and standing up on it. "A couple of weeks ago, one of the companies sent me this really great stuff as a sort of a bonus thing. Let me see if I can find it," she said, putting her entire head into the top part of the cabinet. Jazz giggled. She didn't think Ro's hair was going to fit. "I haven't even had a chance to use it yet," Ro continued. "No one who comes in here ever wants to try anything really wild. Ah, here it is," she finally said, pulling down a shoebox.

Ro climbed down off the stool and took the lid off the box. All the Parrots gathered around and peered inside.

"It's called Body Glitter," Ro explained. "But you can use it anywhere, on your clothes, in your hair, on your skin. It's very glamorous, you'll see. It gives you a little extra sparkle."

Inside the box were several tubes of what looked like different colors of glitter. Ro squeezed some out onto her finger. It was silver.

"This is awesome," Andrea said, reaching for a tube.

Ro brightened. "Oh, Jazz," she said. "I know the perfect thing for that blonde hair of yours. Try some of the gold. It'll really make your hair sparkle."

Jazz jumped into a chair in front of Ro. "Cool," she

said. "I definitely want to try that."

Ro spun Jazz's chair around so that she faced the mirror. Then Ro squeezed some of the gold glitter into the palm of her hand and rubbed it into Jazz's hair.

"There!" she said a moment later. "All done. That looks great! The most important thing to remember about something like this is not to use too much. Subtle is the key to beautiful."

Jazz peered at her reflection. She had no idea what Ro was talking about—all she knew was that her hair looked just the way it always did—wavy and long and blonde.

"You can really see the sparkle when the light hits it," Ro explained, picking up the manicure lamp and shining it on Jazz's hair.

Suddenly Jazz's blonde hair exploded into a mass of twinkling gold sparkles. She gasped. She had never seen anything like it. Ro was right—the glitter looked great. But Jazz couldn't help wondering if maybe a little more would make it look better. As it was, unless a light was shining on it, you could barely see it. And Jazz wanted to make sure that she looked totally glamorous for the roller skating party—and Mike Boxer.

Breezy picked up one of the other tubes of glitter and looked at the label. "You can really use this stuff on your face, too?" she asked.

"Sure!" Ro told her. "It's in a sort of cream base. You just put it wherever you want it."

Breezy carried the tube over to the mirror with her.

"Ooh," said Kim, who had discovered a drawer full of lipsticks. "Look at these."

Suddenly Breezy turned triumphantly from the mirror.

"Well," she said. "What do you think?"

They all looked at the green blob of glitter on her forehead. At first, no one said anything.

"Oh, now I get it!" said Ro after a moment. "It's a baseball field. See how it's kind of a diamond shape?"

Breezy smiled happily. Jazz shook her head. Her cousin was kind of weird sometimes. A baseball diamond?

"I guess I need some of that stuff, too, now," Terry said with a shrug. She applied some pink sparkles to her cheeks.

Kim turned from the mirror and smiled. Jazz almost gasped. Kim had put on some orange lipstick. With her bright red hair and hot pink nails, she looked as if she could glow in the dark.

"Well, I guess it wouldn't hurt to try some of that sparkle stuff, if it really washes out," Crystal finally said.

"I promise!" said Ro, pulling Crystal over by the arm. "I think we should put a little copper on your cheeks. It'll really highlight those cheekbones."

Jazz looked at Crystal. With her amazing height and bone structure, Crystal could probably be a model someday, too, thought Jazz. Jazz decided to go for it. She picked up the gold glitter and squeezed some into her hair and rubbed it around. When she looked up, her mouth dropped open in surprise. Her hair was glowing as if it was radioactive or something.

"Wow!" Kim exclaimed. "You look like an alien."

"Oops!" Jazz blurted. "I guess I got a little carried away."

"I like it," Terry commented with a grin, tweaking a strand of Jazz's sparkling hair.

"I told you to take it easy with that stuff," Ro said, turning to Jazz. She flopped into a chair and smiled at the Parrots. "Here we are, all dressed up with no place to go. I say let's all go out somewhere. Where should we go?"

Suddenly Jazz remembered. "Oh, my gosh," she gasped before she could stop herself, "Rockin' Rollers!"

Ro looked at her in surprise. "Great idea, Jazz," she said. "The roller rink. It'll be my treat! You all played a great game today. You deserve it."

"Cool!" Kim exclaimed.

"Great idea, Jazz," Breezy said.

"Oh, no!" Jazz exclaimed. "I mean, uh, I didn't mean that we should go to the roller rink." What was she going to do now? Everyone was looking at her, waiting for her to say something. And they all wanted to go to the roller rink. But they couldn't! Lindsay was there having her big party.

"What did you mean, then?" Crystal asked.

Jazz searched wildly for an explanation. None came to her. "Well, I . . . I . . . It's just that I kind of have to get going, now. That's what I meant to say," she finished lamely.

"What are you talking about?" Terry demanded. "Where do you have to go?"

"You can't leave now!" Ro exclaimed. "Not when

we're going roller-skating."

"Really," Crystal pointed out. "You're the one who suggested it."

"No," Jazz said, frantically searching for a way to keep them away from the roller rink. "I mean I didn't mean to say that. I definitely don't think you should go roller-skating."

They all looked at her, and she stumbled on, backing out of the room as she spoke. "Actually, I don't even know why I said that. And I really do have to go now. You see, I'm totally tired out from the game today," she explained, rambling on and on. Then she faked a yawn.

"Well, O.K.," Ro said reluctantly. "If you gotta go, you gotta go. I'll walk you to the door. And then when I get back, the rest of us can have a vote. It doesn't have to be Rockin' Rollers. We could go bowling, or we could stay here and watch a movie. I have all the classics on tape. *Godzilla, The Creature From The Black Lagoon.* And we could make popcorn." Jazz knew that Ro was a real monster-movie fanatic. She had a huge collection of old horror movies, and had probably watched each one of them at least five times.

"That's O.K., Ro," Jazz said quickly, hurrying toward the front door of the salon. "I can let myself out."

As soon as she got outside, Jazz started running and didn't stop until she got to the baseball field. She had no idea how late it was, but she knew she had to hurry. She just hoped her bag was still there under the bleachers where she had left it.

All of the lights on the field were off, and it was very

dark. Jazz crawled under the bleachers and felt around for her bag. Luckily, it was still there.

She looked around and realized that the only place to change was right there under the bleachers. She hoped that no one came by. But there didn't seem to be anyone around.

She slipped out of her shorts and T-shirt and pulled the pink polka-dot dress over head. It was a little big, but it would have to do. Oh, no, Jazz suddenly thought— shoes.

Jazz couldn't believe it. She had forgotten to pack her shoes! Now what was she going to do? She didn't have time to run home and get them. There was no way around it, Jazz thought. She was going to have to wear her grubby old sneakers to the party. They probably looked really queer with this fancy outfit, but there was no time to worry about that now. She just had to get to Rockin' Rollers as fast as she could and just hope that no one noticed before she got into her skates!

6

"Eeeeek!" Lindsay screamed as Jazz walked into Rockin' Rollers. Jazz wondered frantically what was wrong. Did she look that scary? Why in the world was Lindsay screaming?

Then Jazz noticed that Lindsay and Beth were trying to get away from Sean. He was shaking a can of soda and chasing them with it.

"Sean!" Beth whined.

"Get that thing away from us!" Lindsay yelled, skating by without noticing Jazz. Jazz collapsed on a bench, exhausted from running all the way to Rockin' Rollers.

Jazz looked up at them and hoped that her pink dress with the bows, which Lindsay was wearing, wasn't going to end up with soda all over it.

"Help!" the two girls shrieked, trying to hide behind Joey. "Stop him!"

Joey grabbed for the can of soda, and the two boys began wrestling for it. Meanwhile, the two girls made their escape and flopped down on the bench beside Jazz. Jazz breathed a sigh of relief that her dress had survived. She had only worn it once, after all.

"Oh, hi, Jazz," Lindsay said, suddenly noticing her. "You're here."

"Hi, Lindsay," Jazz replied. "I'm sorry I'm so late, it's just that . . ." Her voice trailed off. She couldn't think of anything to tell Lindsay. She couldn't very well say that she was at a barbecue at the Pink Parrot.

Lindsay flipped her blonde hair over her shoulder. "Oh, don't worry about it, believe me," she said obnoxiously. "Actually, I had almost forgotten you were coming. It's just too bad for you that you missed so much of the fun."

"Really," Beth echoed. "The last song was a girls' choice. It was great!"

"It was, wasn't it?" Lindsay agreed. "Each girl had to find a boy and ask him to skate." She rolled her eyes at Beth and they both leaned against each other, giggling. "I skated with Joey, of course."

Jazz wondered if Mike Boxer was there. She didn't know if she would have had the nerve to ask him to skate with her during the girls'-choice song, but still she couldn't believe that she had missed it.

Then she noticed Lindsay and Beth looking down toward the floor. She glanced down and saw what they were looking at—her sneakers! How stupid she must look in that dress with those sneakers on. Why hadn't she gotten some skates as soon as she walked in?

"Well, Jazz," Lindsay commented, raising her eyebrows. "Those are way cool shoes you have on."

Beth put her hand up to her mouth to hide a snicker, and Jazz tried to cover up one foot with the other one.

"What's with your hair?" Lindsay asked. "It's, like, glowing in the dark."

"And your dress is the same exact pink as mine," Lindsay continued. "I mean, couldn't you do something besides copy me?"

Before Jazz could say anything, Lindsay jumped up. "Oh, Gwen! Gwen, wait! I wanted to tell you something!" she called, pulling Beth behind her. As the two girls skated off, Lindsay turned her head back towards where Jazz was sitting on the bench. "Jazz, if I were you, I'd go get some roller skates as soon as possible!" she called.

Jazz's cheeks burned. She felt stupid and embarrassed about her sparkling hair and sneakers and stuff, but more than anything else, she felt angry. How could Lindsay say that about *her* pink dress? Jazz had been the one who was nice enough to lend it to her in the first place.

Once her skates were laced, Jazz stood by the edge of the rink and watched the crowd of skaters gliding by. Colored lights flashed on and off, and a mirror ball hung from the ceiling, sending tiny spinning reflections all over the room. Lindsay and Joey were skating together hand in hand. Somehow, Jazz just didn't feel like skating yet. She decided to find the refreshment room and get a soda.

As Lindsay had promised, there was a special private party room in the roller rink just for her guests. Silver and gold streamers and balloons hung from the ceiling, and a big table with a silver tablecloth in the center of the room held cans of soda and bowls of chips.

Jazz went straight for the refreshment table and took a can of soda. Around the room, groups of kids stood talking and laughing.

"Hey, Jazz!" a boy said, tapping her on the shoulder. Jazz turned around and saw Peter Tolhurst grinning at her. He had obviously just walked away from a group of guys standing in the corner of the room. He hung out with the major jocks at Eleanor Roosevelt. "Your hair looks cool!"

"Hi, Peter," Jazz replied, putting her hand to her head and blushing. "I didn't know you were coming to this party." She hadn't really thought about anyone else who might be at the party—just Mike Boxer.

"Yeah, well, I think I'm probably going to go soon."

"Really?" said Jazz, picking up a soda. "You're not having fun?"

Peter shrugged. "I don't know. We're kind of bored," he said, gesturing toward the group of guys behind them. "Hey, that was a great game today. So, you guys are two and one, now, huh? Breezy was something, wasn't she? Seven strikeouts, and she didn't even give up a hit!"

Jazz looked at Peter. He sure did remember a lot about the Pink Parrots' games, and especially about Breezy, Jazz thought. *She* didn't know what their record was or how many strikeouts Breezy had. Peter's crush on Breezy seemed to be getting more serious.

Just then, Jazz noticed Mike Boxer pass by the door to the party room with Joey.

"I think maybe I'm going to go skate or something," Jazz said quickly. Now that she had seen Mike, she didn't want to lose him in the crowd. She put down her soda and skated quickly out of the room.

"Sure, see you later," Peter called after her.

When Jazz got back to the main area, she saw Mike and Joey standing by the edge of the rink. They were leaning on the railing and watching the skaters. Being very careful to act as if she wasn't headed anywhere in particular, Jazz made her way over to where they were standing. Unfortunately, just as she got there, Sean rolled by, snatched Mike's cap off his head and skated away with it. The next thing Jazz knew, Mike was out on the rink chasing Sean, and she was left alone with Joey.

"Well, look who's here!" Joey teased. "One of Hampstead's famous girl baseball players!"

Jazz tried to smile.

"You're not still on that dumb excuse for a team, are you?" he asked her when she didn't answer.

"Well, uh, sort of," Jazz admitted reluctantly. "I mean, I did sign up for the season." She hoped Joey would talk about something else. She didn't really feel like talking about the Pink Parrots.

Joey laughed. "Believe me," he said, "there's no way that team is even going to last the season. Girls aren't supposed to play sports. That's why they're cheerleaders."

Jazz was saved from saying anything when Mike came skating back, putting his cap back on his head and grinning. Her heart began to flutter just looking at him.

"Good! You got it back," Joey said.

"Yeah," Mike agreed. "Sean is a total dweeb." He looked at Jazz and smiled. "Oh, hi, Jazz. I like your . . . um . . . hair."

"Whoa!" Joey cut in before Jazz could answer. "It's kind of blinding if you ask me."

Lindsay skated by just then with Molly, Gwen, Beth and Tory Hibbs, a petite girl with a short brown pixie hair cut who Jazz didn't know very well.

"Hey, Linz!" Joey barked out when he saw her. Lindsay left her group and skated over to the railing, with Tory following her.

"Yes, Joey?" Lindsay said in her sweetest voice.

"Hi, guys," Tory added. "Hi, Mike."

"Come on, let's skate," Joey suddenly said, taking Lindsay's hand and pulling her out onto the rink.

Jazz was left with Mike and Tory. She tried to think of something to say, but her mind was blank. She really had to pay more attention to those magazine articles she read about how to get a guy to talk. Mike looked from Jazz to Tory and back to Jazz. "Well, I think I'll go get something to drink," he said finally, skating off toward the party room.

Tory shrugged and stepped back onto the rink. Jazz figured she'd better skate, too, and followed the others.

It had been at least a year since Jazz had last been skating, and at first she had some trouble keeping her balance. But after the first few shaky moments, it began to get easier. Soon she was gliding along with the rest of them.

She skated around the rink a couple of times. The rink was playing great dance music, and the flashing lights and mirrored ball made everything sparkle. It was O.K., but not exactly fun since Jazz didn't have anybody to skate with.

"Can we skate together?" a guy suddenly asked from behind her, as if he had read her mind.

Jazz turned her head and saw Mike, skating right behind her. She was so surprised that she started to lose her balance. Mike grabbed her by the elbow, grinning. His brown eyes sparkled and Jazz felt her knees turn to jelly.

"Wow, looks like I made it here just in time," he said, holding cut his hand for her to take just as the music slowed down.

Jazz put her hand in his and felt her stomach do a somersault. She couldn't believe she was actually skating with Mike—and holding hands! This had to be a dream. As they glided along, the lights swirled around them. Jazz was in heaven.

Mike turned to look at her. He looked great in the purple shirt he was wearing.

"Jazz," he began. "Can I ask you something?"

Jazz nodded, and felt some major butterflies in her stomach.

Mike brought his face closer to her and squinted. "What's all that shiny stuff in your hair?" he asked. "I like it and everything, but I've never seen anything like it before."

She tried desperately to think of some explanation she

could give Mike. But nothing came to mind.

"Oh, that!" she said, as if a head full of gold glitter were nothing at all. "Well...um...you see, I was helping my little sister Meg with an art project for school, and I guess I got some of the stuff in my hair." She looked up at him to see if he believed her. Jazz thought it was a pretty good story.

Mike laughed. "Boy, that must have been some project," he said. "What were you trying to make, a chandelier?"

Jazz laughed with him. At least he believed her, she thought. Then she gasped. Over by the skate desk were Ro, Breezy, Kim, Terry, Crystal and the rest of the Pink Parrots! "What's wrong?" Mike asked her. He slowed up a little bit. "Did you hurt yourself?"

Jazz didn't even hear him. She was too busy panicking. What if they saw her here after she had told them she was going home? Maybe they weren't really going to skate, she thought. Maybe they would just turn around and leave. She craned her head as she and Mike rounded the far corner. But there they were, getting their skates on. And they were still covered with glitter and colored hair spray.

There was only one thing to do, Jazz decided. She had to get off the rink before they saw her.

"I'm getting really tired," Jazz said, turning toward Mike. "Is it O.K. if we just get off over here for a minute?" She led him toward the opening in the railing that was farthest from the skate desk and the Parrots.

"Sure," Mike agreed, following her to a bench. "But I

thought you were supposed to be one of those athletic girls. Aren't you on that crazy girls' baseball team, the Pink Puffs, or whatever they're called?"

"Well, sort of," Jazz admitted. The negative things that Joey and Lindsay always said about girls playing sports ran through her mind. Mike probably agreed with Joey and Lindsay, even though guys like Peter obviously didn't. Jazz added a tiny little white lie. "I really hardly ever play with them anymore, though."

Mike smiled at her. Jazz almost melted in her seat. He had such a great smile. And that dimple! "That's good," he said. "I can't really understand why a girl would want to play baseball, anyway. It really is a boys' game, you know."

Jazz smiled back at him. "Yeah," she agreed. She'd agree with anything he said as long as he kept smiling at her.

Just then Jazz saw Terry fly by on the rink. She was very unsteady on her skates, and Crystal was pulling her.

"Whoaaaaaa!" Terry yelled, her rainbow-streaked hair flying behind her.

"Hey," said Mike, suddenly, pointing, "isn't that fat girl on your baseball team?"

Jazz tried to pretend that she hadn't seen Terry. "I'm not sure," she said, squinting. "Which one?"

Mike laughed. "How could you miss her!" he cried. "Look at that hair! What did she do to it?"

He turned back to Jazz and began looking at her hair more closely. Jazz backed away. She knew she had to get out of there right away. If any of the Parrots saw her, it would be all over. "Um, I'm going to the bathroom for a minute," Jazz told Mike, wishing frantically that she was anywhere else in the world. She couldn't believe it. She was finally alone with Mike Boxer and here she was running off to the bathroom! "I guess I'll see you in a little while."

Mike shrugged as if it didn't matter one way or the other to him. "O.K.," he said. "See you."

Jazz waited until Mike skated back onto the rink. Then she crouched down a little. She definitely didn't want any of the Parrots to see her now. "Jazz!" a gruff voice suddenly exclaimed. "What are you doing here?"

Jazz stood up and found herself face to face with Terry. "Um . . . I . . . uh . . ." Jazz stammered. She could feel her entire face turning red.

"I thought you said you were tired," Terry accused, her green eyes bearing into Jazz's blue ones. "I thought you also said that you didn't want to go roller skating."

Jazz just stood there, her feet glued to the floor, feeling totally and utterly terrible.

"Ja-azz," Lindsay yelled as she skated over to where Jazz and Terry were standing. "Where've you been? We've been looking for you."

Jazz didn't say anything. Things were worse than terrible now.

"This is *my* party, you know," Lindsay said, frowning at Terry. "So why don't you and your other baseball geek friends just leave us alone?"

Terry glared at Jazz for one more minute and then skated off without another word.

Jazz didn't know what to do, so she did what she usually did when she didn't know what to do—nothing. Lindsay skated off to find Joey while Jazz made her way around the back of the rink, hiding behind the railing. Breezy and Kim had come out onto the rink and were chasing each other around, but it looked as if none of the team had seen her. The exit was right ahead of her and Jazz headed straight for it.

Back outside in the parking lot, she realized that on top of everything else that had gone wrong, there was something else that felt even worse. She looked down at her feet and realized that she was still wearing the Rockin' Rollers' skates! In her rush to get out of there, she had forgotten to turn them in and get her sneakers back. Now what was she going to do? If she didn't return them, she'd get in trouble. Besides, there was no way she could skate all the way home.

There was only one thing to do. She had to sneak back in and return the skates.

Jazz went back inside and practically crawled as she made her way to the skate desk. The man behind the desk gave her a funny look when he saw her stooping, but he handed her back her sneakers. She slipped them on, not even bothering to tie them.

She decided to peek out onto the rink to see if Terry had told all of the Parrots that she was a traitor. But the first thing she saw was Mike Boxer. He was skating with Tory Hibbs, and they were holding hands!

Jazz felt something drop in her stomach. She couldn't believe her eyes. It certainly hadn't taken Mike very long to find another skating partner. And she had felt sorry about leaving him there alone like that!

Jazz stood up, not caring who saw her anymore. She ran out of the rink as fast as she could. She didn't even stop in the parking lot to tie her sneakers, because she was afraid that if she stopped running, she might start to cry.

7

"Yuck! Franks and beans again!" Lindsay said, wrinkling her nose and sticking out her tongue.

"Disgusting!" Molly whined.

"Totally," Jazz agreed, putting silverware on her tray and stepping into line behind the other two girls.

A few people ahead of them, Sean began to bang his knife and fork against his tray and chant in a loud voice, "Beans, beans, they're good for your heart, the more you eat—"

"Sean!" Lindsay practically shouted, cutting him off. She turned to Jazz and Gwen. "I can't believe how incredibly immature he is sometimes!"

"I know," Molly agreed. "Did you see how wild he was acting at your party on Saturday?"

Gwen, who had just joined them, placed her silverware on her tray. "Oh, Linz," she said, "I thought your party was the coolest ever!"

"Totally fun," Beth agreed.

Jazz nodded, even though it had probably turned out to be one of the worst nights of her life. Mainly, she was relieved that no one had noticed how quickly she had left the roller skating rink that night.

Gwen chattered on, tucking a strand of her curly brown hair behind her ear. "So, Lindsay," she said, "my mom's going to call your mom to find out about how you got that special room in the rink and everything, because I might have my birthday party there in the fall."

"It *was* a cool party, wasn't it?" Lindsay said, moving forward with the line and looking over the selection of drinks in front of her. She pouted. "Why can't they ever have anything good for a change, like mineral water or something?" she complained, sighing and placing a container of apple juice on her tray.

Jazz shrugged and chose chocolate milk, her favorite. "Maybe I'll have my birthday party at Rockin' Rollers, too," she said.

"I loved the way the room was decorated, with all those silver and gold balloons and stuff," Molly added.

"Yeah," Beth agreed, nodding. "That was really great."

"I know," Lindsay replied, grudgingly accepting a plate of franks and beans and putting it on her tray. "But next time I have a party there, I'm going to tell them to close the rink. I mean, it was awful, did you see? There were all these regular people there skating around who weren't even invited to the party."

"I know," Molly agreed. "That *was* bad."

Lindsay went on. "The worst part was when those horrible girls from the Pink Parrots showed up with all that stupid makeup and stuff on," she said angrily. "They practically ruined my party!"

"Really," Gwen replied. "Did you see that girl Terry with all that gross colored stuff in her hair? Was that the worst?"

"Definitely," Lindsay agreed. "But Terry looks pretty terrible, even without all that stuff in her hair. I mean, have you ever seen an elephant on roller skates before?" At this, Lindsay, Beth, Gwen and Molly exploded with laughter. They leaned against each other and practically dropped their trays.

Jazz started laughing with Lindsay—because that was what she always did. But her smile faded as she thought about how much she liked Terry, and she felt bad about the way they were talking about her friend. Jazz didn't know what to say, especially since Terry and the other Pink Parrots had not really spoken to her since Saturday night. Jazz felt terrible about the whole thing, but she was at a total loss about how to make up with them. She didn't know how things had gotten so complicated.

They had reached the dessert section, and Lindsay was looking over the bowls of green Jell-O, wrinkling her nose. Jazz liked green Jell-O. She couldn't understand why Lindsay didn't. Suddenly, Jazz realized that someone was staring at her. She turned her head a little and saw Terry standing a few people behind her on line, looking right at her.

Terry was holding a tray loaded with food. Her full face had turned bright red, and she was shaking. She didn't say anything, just bit her lower lip and continued to look at Jazz. Her eyes were very shiny, and she looked as if she was about to cry. Jazz couldn't believe it. She didn't think Terry ever cried—about anything.

Jazz felt terrible. Terry's words from a week ago in the diner echoed through her head: "If you have to say something nasty about someone, you should at least have the guts to say it to his face!" Jazz wished she could go back in time and make it so that the whole conversation on the lunch line had never happened, and that she had never lied to the Parrots about Lindsay's party. She felt really sorry and really upset and Jazz had no clue how to fix the situation. Jazz turned back to Lindsay and tried to forget the whole thing.

Jazz walked as slowly as she could toward the field. All morning she had had a very nervous feeling in her stomach that she couldn't get rid of. It was Saturday, and the Pink Parrots were playing against Dew Drop Inn. Jazz was finally going to have to face Terry.

After what had happened in the lunch line, the two girls had successfully avoided each other all week. Jazz missed Terry and the rest of the Parrots, but they obviously didn't want to be friends with her anymore. She just wished everybody would forget about the whole scene at Rockin' Rollers and things would go back to the way they used to be.

The first person Jazz saw when she got to the field was Crystal. She was sitting on the bench, her nose in a book.

"Hi, Crystal!" she said in a voice that seemed much

too loud and cheerful. "What's that you're reading?"

Crystal held the book up for Jazz to see. The title was *Batter Up! 50 Ways to Improve Your Swing.*

"Looks interesting," Jazz said, trying to make conversation. But Crystal had already gone back to her reading.

Ro was out on the field, signaling everyone to come back to the bench. Jazz had even missed the team warm-up. Jazz watched as Terry tossed a ball to Breezy and headed back to the dugout with the others.

As Terry approached the dugout, Jazz looked hopefully at her. Maybe Terry had forgotten about the whole thing. Maybe if Jazz just pretended that nothing had happened, Terry would, too.

But Terry acted as if she hadn't even seen Jazz and went all the way to the other side of the bench to sit down.

Jazz bit her lip. It didn't seem that Terry had been able to forget about what had happened.

Just then, Kim came jogging back to the Parrots' bench and sat down between Jazz and Crystal.

"Hi, Kim!" Jazz greeted her, trying to pretend nothing was wrong. "Great day, huh?"

"I guess," Kim answered, shrugging.

Jazz hated silences, especially when they were because of her. She took a deep breath, looked around, and tried to think of something to say.

Luckily, Ro started her talk then. But Jazz didn't hear a word she said. She was too busy thinking about Terry. In fact, she probably wouldn't even have noticed that the game was about to start if she hadn't felt someone shaking her.

"Hey!" Ro exclaimed, grabbing Jazz's arm. "Wake up! We have a game to play," she said, staring at Jazz with her deep hazel eyes.

"Oh!" said Jazz, jumping up and realizing that she was the only one left on the bench. In the distance, she saw the rest of the Pink Parrots taking their places out on the field. "Sorry, Ro. I guess I was just thinking."

Ro smiled. "That's O.K.," she said. "Whatever it is, I'm sure you'll work it out. Here!" she called, throwing Jazz her glove, "Don't forget this."

As Jazz trotted out to her position in rightfield, she hoped Ro was right.

Sean Dunphy was the first batter up for Dew Drop Inn. He walked up yawning, as if he were completely bored by the challenge of playing the Parrots. Before stepping into the box, he turned back toward his team's bench and began flapping his arms and squawking, imitating a parrot. The whole Dew Drop Inn team broke out in laughter. Jazz saw Breezy scowl fiercely at Sean. Her first pitch was so fast that it probably burned a hole in Terry's glove.

Jazz tuned out in rightfield. She had to figure out what she was going to say to Terry. She hated having anyone mad at her for so long. Then the crack of a bat hitting a baseball broke into Jazz's thoughts. Sean had hit a routine ground ball to Kim at shortstop. But Kim had trouble getting a handle on it and she bobbled the ball a bit before she got it under control. Sean made it to first base way before the throw. He stood on the bag and waved his fist in the air triumphantly.

Jazz heard cheering and looked over into the stands. Lindsay, Molly, Beth and Gwen were jumping up and down and screaming.

"All right, Sean!" Lindsay screamed.

For a moment Jazz wished that she could be sitting in the stands. But she couldn't understand why Lindsay would cheer for Sean. She had called him totally immature earlier in the week.

Ross Benson, the shortstop, was up next. Ross hit Breezy's very first pitch straight to Andrea at third base. Andrea was so startled she jumped out of the way and missed the ball. It dribbled out to leftfield. Betsy ran in to get it. But it was too late. Ross was safe on first and Sean had advanced to second.

Jazz saw Breezy shaking her head angrily on the pitcher's mound. Her cousin hated it when anyone got a hit off of her. Sam "The Man" Bell came swaggering up to the plate. He was a big, bruising guy who looked more like he should be playing football than baseball.

Jazz started thinking about her problem again. As long as the ball didn't come out to her, she'd be all right. As confused as she felt right now, there was no way she was going to remember how to field the ball—as Terry had taught her. Jazz didn't know what to do about Terry. She had never been in a situation like this before. No one ever got mad at her for very long—except Breezy. But that was different.

"Way to go, Sam!" Lindsay yelled from the stands. Jazz looked up in time to see Sam jogging around the field. She looked around the field but couldn't find the ball anywhere. She wondered where he had hit it.

"Great home run!" Beth called out.

Jazz groaned as she glanced up at the scoreboard. The Parrots were losing by three now. She hated it when they lost, because everyone was in a bad mood then. Baseball was so much more fun when they won.

Jazz started to pay attention. If she did, maybe they'd win. Now Chris Barclay was up for Dew Drop Inn. He fouled the second pitch off high into the air on the third base side. Breezy ran over from the mound, looking up. Terry threw off her mask and ran toward it, too. Her eyes never left the ball. The two girls were getting dangerously close to each other, and Jazz thought for sure they were going to bump into each other. And they did, right as the ball came down. They both fell on the ground.

Miraculously, Terry had the ball in her glove and waved it into the air while on the ground.

Jazz took a deep breath, relieved. Now they only needed two more outs. Something must have happened to Breezy when she fell, because the next six pitches were blazing strikes. Jazz almost smiled when she trotted back to the bench behind the rest of the team. The first half of the inning was finally over, and Dew Drop Inn had a three-run lead. Now it was the Parrots' turn at bat.

Jazz sat down a few feet away from Terry and looked cautiously over at her. But Terry was concentrating intensely on taking off her catcher's equipment, as if she had never done it before.

"That was a really great catch," Jazz said, but Terry acted as if she hadn't even heard her. Jazz turned away, too embarrassed to say anything else.

Breezy was the first batter up for the Parrots. She walked up to the plate, swinging the bat to loosen up. Sean, the pitcher, paused a moment to show her the nasty expression on his face and went into his windup.

The first pitch was a strike. Jazz crossed her fingers in the dugout. She really wanted the team to win the game. Breezy stroked the second pitch to short rightfield for a single. Jazz and the other Parrots cheered from the bench as Breezy crossed first base.

Crystal was up next. She caught a piece of the first pitch and blooped it to third base. Andy Gable, the third baseman, scooped up the ball as if he had all day and threw it to second base. Breezy slid in and beat the ball by a nanosecond. Jazz held her breath until the umpire screamed, "Safe!"

With no outs, and Crystal on first base and Breezy on second, it looked as if the Parrots were in good position to catch up.

Kim walked up to the batter's box swinging the bat furiously. She seemed determined to make something happen.

Sean's first pitch was right down the middle, but Kim swung and missed. She watched the next pitch go by. "Ball!" the umpire shouted.

"Good eye!" Ro called from near first base.

Kim connected solidly with Sean's fastball. It flew out to centerfield. Jazz crossed her fingers again. After all, it had worked before with Breezy. But Sam Bell, moving a lot quicker than Jazz thought he could, caught the ball on the run and triumphantly tossed it back to Sean.

With one out, and Breezy and Crystal still on first and second, Terry came up to bat. She walked slowly to the plate and took a practice swing. Jazz could tell that Terry was out for blood. She had on her "monster look." She looked as if she wanted to take the skin off the ball.

Terry, however, only got a piece of the first pitch. She hit the ball right to Andy. He grabbed the ball, stepped on the bag and then rifled the ball to first. It was a picture-perfect double-play that ended the inning.

Scowling, Terry walked back to the bench to put on her equipment. Jazz knew better than to say anything to her right then.

The first inning was over. The Parrots had tried, but they still trailed Dew Drop Inn 3-0. As they took the field again for the second inning, Jazz was really disappointed. She didn't want the whole team to be in a worse mood than they already were. It was pretty depressing.

Breezy seemed to be in a groove, Jazz thought. She led the inning off with six consecutive strikes. That was 12 in a row, if you counted the last inning. Jazz began to feel a little better. Maybe things were turning around after all. She tried really hard to keep her concentration on the game.

Then Andy was up. Breezy zipped in two quick strikes. But on her third pitch, Andy hit a high fly ball that headed straight toward Jazz in rightfield.

Jazz knew that everyone's eyes were on her. She was determined to show Terry that she remembered all her coaching. Jazz looked up and saw the ball hurtling through the air toward her. She held her glove out in front of her and began to run in the direction of the ball, hoping that it would just fall right in. If she could only make this catch, Terry and the rest of the Parrots might realize how hard she was trying and forgive her. When it seemed as if the ball was directly over her, she clenched her teeth and stuck out her glove, hoping. But she must have tripped or something, because the next thing she knew, she was sprawled on the grass. The ball had dropped somewhere behind her, and Sarah, the Parrots' centerfielder, was running after it. Jazz got up and looked toward the infield just in time to see Andy rounding third. Terry was throwing her mitt in the dirt in disgust.

Breezy got the next batter out, 1-2-3. But it was too late. Dew Drop Inn got another run. The score was now 4-0. Jazz felt as if it was all her fault.

And it didn't get much better. Dew Drop Inn scored its fifth run when Ross Benson hit a solo homer in the fourth (no one else was on base). It didn't help the Parrots' spirits at all to watch him trot around the bases, shaking his fist in the air.

Finally, it was the bottom of the sixth and final inning. With the score at 5-0, the Parrots already had two outs and there didn't seem to be much hope left for them.

Now it was Jazz's turn at bat. She picked up her bat and walked over to the batter's box. She wished that anyone else was up but her. She really wanted to get a hit. Then maybe everyone would be so happy with her they would forget about all her other mistakes. But she had only gotten one hit before in her life, and she was very nervous.

Jazz got into her stance, bat poised, and waited as the pitcher went into his windup. The first pitch was a slow ball right over the plate. Jazz shut her eyes and swung with all her might.

"Stir-ike!" the umpire sang out.

Jazz barely saw the second pitch, which came whizzing into the catcher's mitt. She didn't even move. "Stir-ike two!" the umpire called.

Now there were two strikes against her. She knew this next pitch could be her last chance to get a hit.

Jazz steadied herself at the plate and watched as the pitcher went into his windup. The ball never crossed the plate, though. Suddenly she felt a sting on her leg. She had been hit! The ball had only clipped her thigh, but it hurt a little. She rubbed her leg and looked back at Ro, who nodded and waved her on to first base.

Jazz dropped her bat and limped to first, amazed. She had been walked. When she got to first, she smiled at Julie, who was up next. Jazz felt better than she had all day. It was such an incredible feeling to be on base. There was nothing like it in the world.

The crack of the bat brought Jazz back to the present. Julie had hit the ball! Jazz didn't want to get thrown out so she flew to second. She was so intent on making it to second that she didn't even realize that Julie had hit the ball right to Ross at shortstop. He flipped it to second and Jazz was out. She stood there dazed. If she had only been paying attention, she would have slid into second and then she might have been safe.

When Jazz realized what had happened, she couldn't believe it. She really wanted to win the game. Instead, she was the final out. Jazz felt like crying.

Suddenly, she heard a loud squeal from the bleachers. It was Lindsay. "Yay!" she cried.

Jazz walked over to Lindsay. Maybe Lindsay would say something to make her feel better. Sean was already there by the time she got over to her friends.

"Thanks for cheering, guys," Sean said, smiling at all of them. "It wasn't that hard a game, though."

Lindsay giggled. Jazz suddenly felt a little mad. The Pink Parrots were a *good* team. They just had an off day. But she didn't say anything. It was bad enough her team wasn't talking to her. She'd hate it if Lindsay froze her out again.

Jazz looked over at her team's dugout. Everyone seemed so depressed. This had been the worst game ever. The idea of going home alone made her feel awful. She turned to Lindsay and the others.

"Hey," she said in her most cheerful voice. "You guys want to go to the Neptune?"

Lindsay shrugged. "Well, Joey's game doesn't start for another two hours. I don't see why not. But aren't you going to *change* first?" Lindsay asked, wrinkling her nose as she looked down at Jazz's dirty uniform.

"O.K., I guess I'll meet you there," said Jazz, turning to leave. For the first time in her life, she felt as if someone had invited her to her own diner.

8

Eddie Andrews was wiping the counter with a wet cloth when Jazz walked into the Neptune a half hour later. She had rushed home to shower and change.

"Hey, Cinderella, how's it going?" he called out cheerfully, as Jazz sat down on a stool to wait for Lindsay and the others who were obviously in no rush to get there.

Jazz sighed. "O.K., I guess," she said.

"How was the game today? You played Dew Drop Inn, right?"

Jazz twirled on her stool. "Yeah, we played Dew Drop Inn, all right. They creamed us."

"Ah, don't look so depressed about it," Eddie said consolingly. "Even the best teams have to lose sometimes."

"Yeah, but this time it was practically all my fault," said Jazz.

Eddie raised his eyebrows and shook his head. "Hey, you can't think about it that way," he said. "It's never completely any one person's fault. You're a team! That's what teamwork is all about."

Jazz sighed. The Parrots hadn't exactly been a model

of teamwork that day.

Eddie grinned. "Hey," he said. "I know just what you need. How about one of my Super Sonic Bionic Surprise Milkshakes?"

Jazz couldn't help smiling. Eddie was famous around Hampstead for his incredible ice cream creations. He called them all secret recipes, and never let anyone watch what he put in them. And they always turned out delicious.

Jazz hesitated though. She almost didn't want to feel any better. Eddie turned around and grabbed a milkshake glass. "Now, remember, no peeking! Go put some music on or something, so you won't see what I'm putting in it."

"Thanks, Eddie," she said, hopping down off her stool and heading for the juke box against the opposite wall. She didn't want to hurt Eddie's feelings by telling him she didn't want one of his special milkshakes.

Five minutes later, the door to the diner opened, and Lindsay and Beth walked in, giggling.

"Oh, hi, Jazz," Lindsay said. "Ooooh, I don't want to sit at the counter. Let's sit over here, in *my* booth."

Jazz picked up her glass and followed the girls to a booth in the back. For the first time, she wondered why it was so important for Lindsay always to sit in that booth.

"Where's Molly?" Jazz asked.

"Oh, she should be here soon," Beth said. "She had to go home first."

"Ugh!" Lindsay practically screamed, with a horrified

expression on her face. "What is that you're drinking?"

Jazz looked down at her Super Sonic Bionic Surprise milkshake and shrugged. "It's just a milkshake," she said.

"Looks more like a mudshake to me!" Lindsay exclaimed, wrinkling her nose. "I don't even want to know what's in it!"

"Really," Beth agreed, giggling.

Jazz looked around. Eddie was back in the kitchen. She hoped he hadn't heard what Lindsay and Beth had said.

"You know what it really looks like?" Beth said suddenly. "It looks like that ugly sweater that Gwen wore to your party last weekend."

Lindsay burst out laughing. "You're right!" she shrieked. "Wasn't that the worst-looking thing?" She turned to Jazz. "You saw it, didn't you?"

Jazz shook her head. She had been much too busy the night of Lindsay's party to notice anything but her own troubles.

"Oh, it was so tacky!" Lindsay went on. "I can't believe you didn't notice it! I mean, it looked like someone had just taken all the leftover pieces of yarn off the floor and knitted them together to make a sweater."

Jazz started thinking that it was pretty obnoxious of Lindsay to talk that way about someone who was supposedly one of her best friends.

Lindsay brightened suddenly. "Oh, my gosh, Jazz, I can't believe I didn't tell you," she said excitedly. "I have the best news. You are going to be so happy."

"What is it?" Jazz asked, hoping for something that would cheer her up.

"Remember how we couldn't find that dress for me in Serendipity that day?" she asked. Jazz nodded.

"Well," Lindsay continued, "I went back yesterday to see if they had it in yet, and guess what?"

"It was there?" Jazz guessed.

"No, even better!" said Lindsay. "There was a new display, called 'Sugar and Spice,' and I found a dress that's much nicer. Yours is nothing compared to this one."

Jazz started to get mad. How could Lindsay rank on the dress Jazz had been nice enough to lend her and then expect her to be happy that she had gotten a new and supposedly better dress?

"Oh, gosh, Lindsay, that's great!" Beth exclaimed. "What does it look like?"

"Well," Lindsay began. "It's pale peach, which is a great color on me, and it's got this really cute flare mini-skirt that puffs out when you twirl around. But the best thing is there's this little row of pale peach roses, made out of the same material as the dress, that goes all the way around the neck."

"Oh, Linz, it sounds so cute!" Beth gushed.

Jazz didn't say anything. She was thinking about how Lindsay still hadn't returned her own dress to her yet.

The diner door opened, and the little bells hanging on it tinkled. Gwen and Molly walked in.

"Hi, you guys!" Lindsay called.

Jazz was surprised at how friendly Lindsay sounded.

How could she talk that way about Gwen's sweater one minute and act so friendly toward her the next?

"Hi," Gwen said, walking over to their booth. Molly nodded at all of them.

"Hi," Beth said.

Lindsay's eyes opened wide. "Oh, my gosh, Gwen!" she shrieked. "That jumpsuit is so cute! Where did you get it?"

"My aunt sent it to me from Chicago," said Gwen, twirling around so she could model her outfit.

Lindsay looked disappointed. "Oh, I was hoping you got it at the mall or something," she said.

"Linz was just telling us about this great new dress she found at Serendipity," Beth explained. "Tell them about it, Linz."

"Well," she began, "it's pale peach. . . ."

Jazz tuned out. She wasn't sure if she felt like listening to Lindsay talk about her great new dress anymore.

"Maybe I'll ask my mom if she can get me one," Molly said.

"Molly! You can't get the same dress I get!" Lindsay whined. "It wouldn't be fair! After all, I'm the one who discovered it."

"Oh, yeah," Molly said sheepishly. "I guess you're right."

But Lindsay had wanted to get Jazz's exact dress and Jazz hadn't told her she couldn't, Jazz thought. She gritted her teeth so she wouldn't say anything, but she was getting even madder.

Just then, the door to the diner flew open and the

Parrots came in, talking and joking loudly. They headed straight for the two booths by the counter that they usually sat in.

"Oh, great, here come the 'fellas,'" Lindsay joked.

Gwen looked over her shoulder. "Ugh," she said. "Look how dirty they are!"

"And so loud!" Molly added.

"Hey," Lindsay said. "Speaking of loud, did you hear about Mr. Carrera's math class on Thursday?"

"No," said Molly, "what happened?"

"Well, everyone was acting really rowdy," Lindsay explained. "Sean Dunphy actually threw a pencil at Mr. Carrera!"

"I heard about that," said Gwen. "And so then didn't Mr. Carrera get really mad and give the whole class extra homework or something?"

"Five extra pages!" said Lindsay. "But the worst part was, after class, just as we were all leaving, I saw Tory Hibbs walk up to Mr. Carrera and say she was sorry. You should have heard her in her little high voice—'Even though I wasn't involved in it, I want to apologize for the way the class behaved.' It was disgusting!"

Gwen made a face. "She's such a goody-goody," she said.

"Really," Molly agreed.

"Doesn't she just make you sick?" Lindsay asked.

Jazz took a sip of her milkshake. She started noticing that Lindsay did an awful lot of talking about people who weren't around to defend themselves. Tory Hibbs hadn't exactly been Jazz's favorite person because of

113

what had happened with Mike Boxer at Rockin' Rollers. But Jazz had to wonder. Why had Lindsay even invited Tory to the party if she didn't like her?

Just then, Terry got up from the table in the back and walked over to the jukebox. She glanced at Jazz for a moment, but quickly turned away.

Jazz began to think. She had certainly been willing to laugh at jokes about Terry when she thought Terry couldn't hear them. Maybe Lindsay talked about all her friends behind their backs that way. Jazz began to wonder what Lindsay and the rest of them said about *her* when she wasn't around.

Terry's selection began to play on the jukebox. It was Ro's favorite song, the one that she just couldn't resist dancing to. Sure enough, when she heard the music, Ro stood up from the table and began to clap and move her hips to the beat.

Lindsay rolled her eyes. "Have you ever seen anything so unbelievably tacky?" she asked, nodding toward Ro.

"Really," Molly agreed.

"And what about that hair?" Gwen added, making a face.

Jazz looked back toward the Parrots' booths. Ro had pulled Kim up and was trying to get her to dance. Kim's face had turned as red as her hair, and she was trying to get back to her seat. The rest of the Parrots were laughing. They sure seemed to be having a great time, thought Jazz with a pang, especially for a team that had just lost a game.

At that moment, Eddie walked over to the Parrots' table carrying a double cheeseburger with everything on it. He set it on the table where Terry had been sitting.

"Now *that's* disgusting," Gwen announced.

"Gross," Molly agreed.

"They even eat like guys," Lindsay said snidely. Jazz sighed. She was getting a little tired of listening to Lindsay bad-mouth everyone.

The song ended. As Ro and Kim fell back into their seats, laughing, the rest of the Parrots cheered and began slapping the two of them on the shoulders.

"Can't they even keep quiet?" Lindsay whined. Jazz bit her tongue. She was beginning to wish that *Lindsay* would be quiet.

"Really," Molly agreed.

"How rude!" Gwen added.

Lindsay shook her head. "They shouldn't even be allowed in here," she said haughtily. "Look at them, acting like they own the place!"

Jazz turned to her. "Listen, Lindsay," she said, "my family *does* own this place!"

Lindsay gaped at her in surprise.

Jazz couldn't stop herself. She couldn't even think about what she was saying. She just said it. She stood up. "I don't think there's anything wrong with the way they're acting! It's a whole lot better than the way you're acting—sitting in the corner watching everyone who comes in here like a hawk!"

Lindsay's face was turning red. Jazz stood up.

"And another thing!" she said, suddenly becoming

aware of the fact that the whole diner had become very quiet. "What's the big deal about girls who play baseball? What do you spend your time doing that's so much better? Talking about your own friends behind their backs? And you still haven't returned the pink dress you borrowed from me to wear to your party!"

Jazz felt every eye in the place on her. The Parrots were staring at her from their table, and Eddie was frozen in his place behind the counter. Beth, Gwen and Molly looked up from the booth, shocked. Lindsay started to shake.

Jazz clenched her fists. "You think you're really great, Lindsay," she said, "but you know what I think you are? I think you're spineless—the way you talk about people when they're not around to defend themselves." She paused and took a breath. "If you have to say something nasty about someone, you should at least have the guts to say it to her face!"

Lindsay's eyes narrowed. "Jasmine Jaffe, you'll be sorry for this!" she said. "I hope you know you've just lost some very important friends!"

Jazz stared right back at her. "I'd rather have no friends at all than be friends with someone like you!" she said, as she left the table. She pulled open the door to the diner with a yank and slammed it behind her so hard that all the bells jangled.

9

"Jasmine, don't just stand there with the door open," Mrs. Jaffe said to her daughter with a sigh. "Either take something to eat or close the fridge."

Jazz blinked. She hadn't realized that she was still staring into the refrigerator. She took a last look around and shut the door.

"I hope you're not just going to mope around here all day," her mother went on. "If you don't have anything to do, why don't you go down to the diner. Your father could probably use the help."

Jazz shook her head. After what had happened in the diner with Lindsay the day before, she felt that she never wanted to go back there again. Besides, she didn't want to take the chance of running into anyone from the team. They were all probably still pretty mad at her. And considering the way she had treated Terry in school and had ruined the game for them on Saturday, Jazz didn't blame them.

She walked over to the kitchen window and looked out at the sky. Jazz had never liked Sundays, and cloudy Sundays were even less fun. But the absolute worst were cloudy Sundays when you knew that everyone in the world was mad at you.

She went back to her room and flopped down on her bed. Meg was sprawled on the floor, her plastic dinosaurs lined up in front of her.

"What are you doing?" Jazz asked, rolling over onto her stomach and looking down at Meg.

"It's the Dinosaur Olympics," Meg explained. "Right now the stegosaurus has to wrestle with the allosaurus." She looked up at Jazz. "Want to play?" she asked. "I'll let you be the tyrannosaurus rex."

Jazz shook her head, and Meg began to make dinosaur fighting sounds. Jazz stood up and sighed. Normally, the sound of Meg's roaring would have really bugged her, but this time she didn't even bother saying anything about it.

She walked over to her dresser and began looking through the bottles of nail polish on her shelves. Maybe she should do her nails. That usually made her feel good. She picked up a bottle of Perfect Pink and carried it over to her bed. She opened the bottle and took out the little brush. But, somehow, she just didn't feel like it after all.

Jazz left Meg and her dinosaurs and went into the living room to see what was on T.V. After flipping the channels, passing by a news program, a game show and a documentary about turtles, she settled on *Godzilla vs. King Kong.*

But after a few minutes, she realized that the show was just reminding her too much of Ro and her collection of old monster movies. She had to turn it off. Jazz sighed.

She was lonely and miserable.

Suddenly, the doorbell rang. Jazz had no idea who it could be, but she ran to answer it, happy to have something to do.

She pulled open the front door, and there, standing on the porch, were Ro, Terry, Breezy, Crystal, Kim, Julie, Betsy, Sarah, Andrea—the whole team! Jazz was so surprised to see them that she just stared, not saying anything.

Terry stuck out her hand and gave Jazz a pink bundle.

"Here," she said. "We thought maybe you might like to have this back."

Jazz unwrapped the bundle. "My dress!" she exclaimed. "But how did you get it?!"

"It was easy!" said Ro, grinning. "We just went over to that girl's house and asked for it."

Jazz's mouth dropped open. "You went to Lindsay's?" she asked, astounded.

"Ro went," Breezy explained. "The rest of us waited around the corner."

"Lucky for me she wasn't home," said Ro. "I had a little talk with her mother, whom I know because she comes to the salon to get her hair done. So I explained that her daughter had borrowed a dress and forgotten to return it. She let me in, and we found it together."

"But how did you know which dress it was?" Jazz asked, still amazed.

"Come on, Jazz," Terry said, laughing. "How could we not know? You were so proud of that thing the day you wore it to school. You showed it to everyone!"

"We just told Ro what to look for," Crystal explained.

Jazz looked at the group of girls on the porch and felt as if she were going to cry.

"You guys are the greatest," she said. "I can't believe you would do this for me. I don't deserve it."

"Sure you do," Kim said.

"After all," Terry added, "Real friends stick up for their friends when they need it."

Jazz smiled. "Do you want to come in?" she asked, opening the door wider and taking a step back.

"I've got a better idea," said Ro. "Let's go to Rockin' Rollers. That way you can make up for all the fun you missed by not coming skating with us that night."

Jazz felt her cheeks turning red. "I know I've been really terrible. Well, there's one thing I'm sure about, though. I don't think I'll be skating with Mike Boxer—or any of Lindsay's friends—anymore." She smiled at them. "Now I know who my real friends are. I'm just lucky you guys are willing to give me another chance."

"Are you kidding?" teased Terry. "We just can't afford to lose your fielding abilities."

Jazz laughed and ran inside to tell her mother she was going out. She was so happy to have her friends back. Finally, she knew who her *real* friends were.

About the Author

B. B. Calhoun

B. B. Calhoun grew up in New York City and still lives in Manhattan with her husband, a painter. She was a teacher and sports instructor at a private school in New York City. This is Ms. Calhoun's third book.

Watch For

MIXED SIGNALS

Number 3 in **THE PINK PARROTS** *series!*

It was the bottom of the sixth and the Parrots last chance to beat Quicky Chicken. The Parrots were down by a score of 6-5, and Terry DiSunno was the first batter up. Iceman, Quicky Chicken's ace pitcher whose trademarks included a black baseball glove and black wrap-around sunglasses, went into his windup. The ball whizzed right up the middle past Terry. Strike one.

"Come on, Terry," Breezy Hawk yelled.

The next pitch was wide, but Terry swung anyway and missed. Strike two.

"Oh, no," Kim Yardley groaned. "She's just got to get a hit! Blast it, Terry!"

Iceman took off his hat and slowly ran his fingers through his hair. Then he smugly shook off his catcher's signal. Terry swung her bat a few times and, scowling fiercely, stepped back up to the plate. Iceman just smiled and went into his windup. His supersonic fastball headed straight for the plate, but Terry was ready for it. Her bat was a blur as she made solid contact and sent the ball soaring out over the centerfielder's head.

"Way to send it, Terry!" Breezy yelled, jumping up and down in excitement in front of the dugout.

Terry's hit finally got the team hustling, and the Parrots then got the two hits they needed to win the game. The Quicky Chicken players were shocked—they almost never lost, especially to a bunch of girls, and *never* when they put Iceman in to pitch. . . .

After the game the Parrots went to the Neptune Diner to get ice cream in celebration of their victory. Then the Quicky Chicken team showed up. Iceman, still wearing his shades, accidentally bumped into Terry, and proceeded to stand there glaring at her as if it was all her fault.

"Got a problem?" Terry asked him obnoxiously through a mouthful of hot fudge. "Besides thinking your fastball is a killer when it's not?"

"I wouldn't talk," Iceman retorted. "You dweebs were just lucky."

Before Terry could make a good comeback, Iceman swaggered away with his teammates following right behind him.

"What a total jerk Iceman is!" Terry complained to Jazz on their way home.

Jazz nodded. "He's really cute, though," Jazz added. "I can totally understand why you like him—"

"LIKE HIM?!" Terry exploded, her mouth hanging open in shock.

"Yeah, Ter," Jazz continued with a knowing half-smile on her lips. "You've got all the symptoms."

"Symptoms?" Terry asked in confusion.

"Uh-huh," Jazz said calmly. "You're having your first major crush, Terry DiSunno. And you couldn't have picked a hotter looking guy!"